EXILE

EXILE

Pádraic Ó Conaire

Translated from the Irish by

Gearailt Mac Eoin

Cló Iar-Chonnachta
Indreabhán, Conamara, Éire

First published by Conradh na Gaeilge as *Deoraíocht*, 1910
First English edition published by Cló Iar-Chonnachta, 1994
© Cló Iar-Chonnachta 1994
Second Edition 1999

ISBN 1 874700 62 1

Cover Artwork: Graham Knuttel

Cover Design: Johan Hofsteenge

Design: Deirdre Ní Thuathail

Cló Iar-Chonnachta receives financial assistance from
The Arts Council / An Chomhairle Ealaíon

**This translation was shortlisted for the
Aristeion Prize for Translation, 1996**

The translator gratefully acknowledges the generous assistance of The School of Irish Studies Foundation towards the completion of this work.

Printing: Clódóirí Lurgan, Indreabhán, Conamara
091-593251/593157

THE AUTHOR

This diminutive man, whose statue sits pensively in the central Square of his native city, was born in Galway in 1882. Orphaned at twelve years of age, he was brought to live with relatives in Ros Muc, in the Connemara Gaeltacht, where he became totally immersed in the delights of the Irish language and its ancient songs and literature, preserved orally through centuries of persecution and censorship from the Colonial Government and of banishment from an educational system which was controlled by the English.

After some years in an ecclesiastical boarding school, he obtained a junior post in the Civil Service in London, and he joined the Gaelic League where his burgeoning literary talent was stimulated and encouraged. Between 1904 and 1913 he won six major literary prizes and, having enlisted in the first battalion of the Irish volunteers in London, returned to Ireland in 1915 to play his part in the armed struggle for independence under the leadership of his Gaelic League colleague, General Michael Collins.

His journalistic and literary output continued to be prodigious although, having sacrificed his Civil Service post, he was forced to spend the rest of his short life as a vagrant in Ireland. Creative writing in the Irish language was even less profitable then than it is today. Moneyed people in Ireland, then as now, loved to meet writers and artists in public houses and to buy them drink, but that was usually the extent of their patronage, and Pádraic became known as a great connoisseur of Irish whiskey, although he rarely had much to eat. He had never been robust and his way of life caused a gradual deterioration in his health.

He died alone in the paupers' ward of a Dublin hospital on the sixth of October, 1928. His sole possessions, apart from his clothing, consisted of a pipe, a piece of plug tobacco, an apple and a pocket knife.

His published work included over 400 short stories, a genre of which he was an undoubted master, several moderately successful plays, hundreds of newspaper and magazine articles on literary and other subjects, and this, his only finished novel.

Although a prose writer, Ó Conaire's genius lay, to a great extent, in his poetic ability to use language itself to evoke, to paint pictures, to delight with rippling cadences of sound. His writing remains a shaft of light — blinding — from the hidden Ireland. Lacrimae rerum?

Gearailt Mac Eoin

THE TRANSLATOR

Gearailt Mac Eoin is a poet, short story writer and literary translator who has won many major awards and has three published collections of poetry. He is joint editor of *Byzantium*, the best-selling bilingual edition of selected poems by William Butler Yeats, and his collection of stories, *Brocairí Bhedlington*, was nominated for the *Irish Times* Literature Prize.

Pádraic Ó Conaire

Chapter One

I had not been more than two and a half years in London at that time, even so, I should not have stayed there much longer than I did — yes, it must be said — had I possessed as much as would have taken me home. But when a person is not employed, and has not more than two pence in his pocket, and without much in his stomach, what can he do?

Oh! Wasn't I the unfortunate that was not killed on that unlucky day when the motor car went over me as I was out looking for work? If I had been killed, I should not now be a poor cripple, at only twenty-seven years of age. I should not be an old heap of flesh, unable to move from one place to another without the crutch, any more than an old forest tree laid low by the axe, I should not be expecting help from all and sundry, with my one leg and my one arm. And the owners of the vehicle that went over me would not have had to pay me two hundred and fifty pounds when I came out of hospital.

How well I remember that day, how full of joy I was to be able to walk, with my crutch and my wooden leg. How miraculous was each stroke struck by the wooden leg on the paving stones of the street. I thought at first that it wasn't I who was making the noise at all. Indeed, I was little affected, what with learning to walk again, and being able to get along under my own steam. I kept moving along all the time, taking great care of myself, sometimes imagining that the crutch might slide away from me, other times telling myself that I was doing extremely well. There was a kind of delight in my heart to be able to make my own way about at all.

It was a fine day of sunshine and the streets were full of people. Some of them carefree, light-hearted, others burdened, sad in themselves. And others seemed timid, anxious, fearful. Every one with his own story to tell , and I myself with my tale of woe. I started to think. I should have to spend the rest of my life in this predicament. I began to hate those people who were passing me by on healthy limbs, so quickly, so full of gusto. I thought they should at least have looked at me, at someone who was learning to walk for the second time, someone who had been face-to-face with death, and had come back again, someone with only one arm and one leg and a twisted, warped and ruined face.

I was angry because nobody noticed me, because nobody asked me for my story, that I was not being asked about my accident; but when a lovely young lady who was passing by looked pityingly at me, and seemed about to speak, my anger turned to rage. She was just being inquisitive, I thought. The flighty butterfly! What could she have to do with anybody like me? I needed to insult her in some way; since I understand well how much people, and especially women, hate cripples like myself, although you might think that they'd have a lot of pity for us. But I managed to hold my tongue until she had passed me by.

I had started listening again to the sound of the wooden leg striking the street, when I saw a boy bowling an iron hoop in front of him. He was a happy-looking well-built lad with curly fair hair, and when he saw the sweat pouring off me, and my general sorry state, he tossed me a penny he had in his fist. It took me some effort not to hit him with my stick. Why should he have thought I needed money? Surely the world's blindest could see that I was on my way to the bank to collect my two hundred and fifty pounds. The boy had pitied me and I hated him for it. Until that moment I had not been aware of the great change which had come over my heart since my accident. The sort of change that comes over a potato left on the ridge under the autumn sun. I suddenly realised that I had become a surly melancholic, and I made a firm resolve to repair the damage if I could.

The lawyer was waiting for me in the bank. He had everything in order. I was getting my two hundred and fifty pounds. They had expected me to leave the money under my name at the bank, but I wouldn't. What size notes would I prefer? Not notes — gold! They were surprised when I said that, but if they had known that there had not been two yellow sovereigns in my pocket at any one time since I left my home and my blood relations, there might not have been such surprise. Anyhow, I got the gold in a bag. They put me sitting in a taxi-cab, and I was not long making my way home.

I went into my room — the hospital people had got me the lodgings. I locked the door. I banged the bag against the wall so as to hear the clink of the gold. I threw it casually on the table, as if I had one like it every day of the year. I sank back into a comfortable chair and watched the bag for a while. I closed my eyes. A sigh escaped from me; then another sigh. I started crying.

When I opened my eyes, I saw the bag on the table, the bag which held the value of one of my arms, one of my legs, and the ruin of my features.

There was magic in that little yellow bag. It was yellow; could it be any other colour, with all that gold inside? I couldn't keep my eyes off it. Night was falling, and everything in the room was going out of perspective; the bed, the table, the other chair, even the walls were gradually disappearing from sight. All I saw was the little yellow bag that contained my share of the world.

I lit a candle. I spilt all the gold out across the table. I started to handle it. I was letting it slip through my fingers the way children let sand slip through their fingers on the beach.

I sensed nothing but the gold. I heard nothing but the sound of it, saw nothing but its colour. If there was anything in my mind at the time, it was only the gold. Thinking about it now, there probably wasn't even that, but the mind was at ease, the ease a mother feels when she knows her child is beside her.

I had covered the little table with gold. Such a tablecloth was never spread before a king. But I wasn't wholly satisfied.

I divided the gold into five heaps, made five castles, fifty sovereigns in each castle. Ten underneath, nine on top of ten, eight on top of nine, and so on until I had the castles built. It suddenly came into my mind that each heap of them would do me for a year. Five years and all would be spent. What should I do then? I began to lose courage. Some move I made sent a sovereign spinning to the floor. "You want to go," I said to it. I took off my coat and spread it over the gold. I called the landlady.

I gave her the sovereign from the floor and asked her to bring me food and drink.

She did so. But my heart was becoming so sad, from thinking about the next five years, and what would happen to me after they were over, that I couldn't taste the food. However, I ate and drank all she had given me, and fell asleep on the chair, still handling the gold, but without taking off a stitch of clothes.

When I wakened in the morning there were not five castles of gold on the table, but rather a golden tablecloth, and the morning sunlight was turning everything in the room to gold.

I lay back on the bed. Opposite me the sunlight was dancing on a small insignificant picture which was fixed to the wall. It was a picture of three young men drinking. The way the sun was shining on them, they seemed to be a merry trio.

I felt that I should like to be in their company. If I were, surely this sadness and heart-weariness would leave me. My mind would no longer be on the wooden leg, or on the one arm, or on my scarred, ruined cheekbones. No. But where were my friends and companions that I could not go to them? Stray, homeless people that they were, I had no hope of seeing them, after my long stay at the hospital. That didn't worry me. So long as I had money I should not be without company.

I got up and went out, carrying the little yellow bag. I stopped at the bank first, and put the money on deposit, all except ten pounds that I kept for spending.

There is a tailor's shop on the other side of the street, across from the bank. I bought a new suit there. As I was coming out, I met a man who said that he had seen my accident happening.

I needed company. I had to have somebody who would talk to me. I went drinking with him, and it wasn't long before I had forgotten about the wooden leg, and about my lost arm, and about the accident itself.

The alchemy of the drink was turning everything into gold.

Chapter Two

When money comes into the possession of a person who has never had any experience of it, it drifts away from him as chaff drifts before the wind. That was the way it was with me. Mine was going, and going fast. Going like river water. However, that did not discourage me. Had I not got good companions? Were they not happy to do everything for me? Was I not now an important person? Was I not able to spend money with any gentleman? Every day the same people were in my company. Every day there was the same spending of money, but it was I who was always spending it. Oftentimes, when I woke up in the morning, I would say to myself, when I saw the wooden leg on the chair, that I would spend no more money on my companions. But I should have been lonely without them.

I used to look at the little picture that hung on the wall in my lodging, at the three young men who were so merry, so high-spirited, whilst the sun shone on them. Then I would fall to thinking on my own pitiful condition. It used to anger me to see the people of the house going up and down the stairs, something that I couldn't do without help. It used to anger me to hear the sound of boots on the street. It would enrage me to see somebody in high spirits, when I was melancholy and depressed. Then I used to remember how affable I could be after a couple of drinks. Was there not a strong God? Why should I be insulting Him by thinking that He would leave me stripped and penniless once I had spent all I now had? That would be a great sin. I would dress and go out.

Bought wisdom is the best of wisdom. I had not bought much of it until I had spent a year in this way — until I was down to eighty pounds. I had become practiced on the wooden leg by this time, and on the new life that had come. Even so, it was often agony for me to see somebody running. I would want to hit him with my crutch, and if I had killed him, I should have been just as pleased. Didn't I knock a young man down one day, as he was passing me by on lithe, athletic limbs, and were they not going to put me into prison? And they would have, only for one of my acquaintances who was there, and who told them my story.

He it was who saved me from prison, and he it was who taught me some sense, and this is the way I was taught: we went drinking, us two, spending money in the usual way. Unfortunately, however, I had forgotten to bring more than a few shillings with me that day. At first he did not seem to believe me. In any event, when I told him, he wasn't prepared to give me the crown piece that I asked him for on loan. He hadn't got the money, if he could be believed. But by the manner in which he turned up his nose at me, I could see immediately that he thought that all my money was spent. After all I had spent on him and on his useless friends!

Anger took hold of me, then frenzy. I called him by every vile name that I could think of. I threatened him with my crutch. All he did was to go into a fit of laughter, mocking me, mocking the fool who had spent his money on him. It came into my mind to split his head open with a large urn that stood on the counter, even if I were to hang for it. I should have done so, too, I was so incensed, only for the landlord, who took the urn to a place of safety.

I left, but as I was leaving, I could hear the people in the public house laughing at me, and at the wooden leg, and telling each other what an ill fellow was this cripple. Seventeen devils were eating at my heart, and if there was ever a murderous man, and one ready to do murder, I was that man.

That night, lying on my little bed, I examined my conscience. I went over every little thing that had happened to me, and everything I had done since I had lost the use of my limbs. I had been realising for some time that a great change had come over my disposition, my heart and my mind; that my mind, in fact, had changed much more than my body; that hatred and disgust, and depression and wretchedness, would be my companions for the future; that I should have gloom for a spouse until the day of my death.

This thought filled my heart with melancholy. I resolved to change my habits, my life, my way of living — to leave the city, or at least to find a place to live far away from my false friends. I calculated how much of the money was left — seventy pounds in the bank and a couple of pounds in the house. Lord! Hadn't I been making a fool of myself? Hadn't I been going down the slippery slope, spending my money with those wretches? And all the time they had been laughing at me!

Truly was I depressed and ashamed of myself. I threw myself on the floor and began to roll from side to side, pulling hair from my head with sorrow and regret. I said a couple of prayers. I vowed in the presence of God that my life for the future would be different, if it was His holy will. Then I began to sob and weep until my beard was wet with tears.

In the morning I told the landlady that I was leaving.

Chapter Three

The next house I stayed in was on the other side of the city and, because of that, I had no fear of meeting any of the old companions. Had I had more money, I should not have stayed in the city at all, but I was still hoping to get some work, some light work that I might be capable of doing.

Anyhow, I settled into the big house, and what a really enormous house it was! When full, there were four hundred men living there. Each man had his own little cubicle. And in the mornings you could see each of them preparing his own bit to eat.

But, even though the crowd in the house was huge, I was lonely there. Lonelier, in a way, among the large crowd, than in my own little room in the old place. I usually preferred to be by myself, and I used to sit by the window, looking out at the street and at the people passing by; at the carriages, the motor cars (they always made me feel angry). Then the loneliness and sadness would get such a grip on my heart that I would have to get up and join the company. But I felt so depressed and unhappy that I used to think they were all laughing at me, that they disliked, even hated me. It seemed to me that they only wanted to evict me from the house. And the ones who were down on their luck (and of these there were many), I imagined that they probably thought the glum cripple was to blame; that it was he who had brought them bad luck.

I would then start remembering all the stories I had heard about sailors who threw the man who brought them bad luck into the sea. Would something like that be done to me? Would it be better for me to leave the place altogether, and to make my way out into the country? But then the city was the only place where I might find suitable work. Why should I leave?

But I shall soon have to leave the house, anyway. My money is running out, slipping away, slipping away, without my noticing. How has so much of it gone in the past three months? I have not been spending any of it foolishly. Certainly not. God knows that. I have been looking twice at every penny before spending it. And why wouldn't I? What would there be to do once it was gone except . . .? I had no answer to that question. Seven times daily, and seventeen times nightly, I had been putting this question to myself, and the only answer I could find was to count what remained of the money, although I well knew how much was there. I used to calculate on a piece of paper how long more it would last me, assuming that I only spent so much every day. If I watched it carefully, it should take me through the spring. But then? Once my money was spent, what would lie in store for me? Oh my God, I am going mad, God help me! God help me!

Not a cloud of sleep drifted over me that night, but if it didn't, it was not because of the money worries, but because of dreadful pains in my shoulders. I suppose the pains are caused by the crutch, but if I don't get a cure for them, I shall not be able to walk a step. I shall have to stay in this great ugly house from morning till night, from Monday to Saturday, from Saturday to Monday, till the day of my death.

When I got up, a man was standing outside the door of the room, and he helped me down the stairs. As we were going into the big room on the ground floor, I noticed a small crowd gathered around the fire at the far end of the room; they were having a discussion. Once they saw me, they put a stop to the talk, and called me over.

I was surprised, because I had hardly ever spoken a word to them. Some of them were workmen. Some of them were looking for work. And as for some of the others, only themselves and God knew how they managed to get anything to eat. And you would not be far wrong if you said that there were thieves and pickpockets among them. The man who had helped me down the stairs spoke to me in a charitable way and said they had business with me.

I was called over again.

I joined their company.

A big burly man stood up and imposed silence on all present. He began to praise me. I had nothing but the kind word for everybody. I never talked behind anybody's back. I never started trouble. I was kind and gentle to all . . .

With the great praise he was giving me, I began to think that there must be nobody like me in the world. He praised me as a poet might praise his lover. And he was a true poet. The language that flowed from him was rough. There were too many swear-words in it. But it came from his heart and moved his audience greatly. I, too, was moved by the speech, and I was surprised indeed when he told the man who had brought me down the stairs to bring me into the centre, and when he came over to us, pushing in front of him a small chair which moved on two big wheels at the back and two small ones at the front.

The big man said that he had seen the chair in a shop; that some of them thought it would suit me nicely; that they had bought it for me; that I should be able to go from place to place in it; nice and easy; that I should be able to make a long journey by this mode of transport without any great effort; that I should do myself good by getting into the chair this minute so that they could all see me.

I got in, and I motored nicely and easily up and down the long room. From the joy and delight that took hold of these homeless men, you would think they were a crowd of youngsters just let out of school. They weren't satisfied until I had travelled up and down the room eight or nine times.

I thanked them all, and off they went, one after another.

It was not long until I was alone in my chair in that big room. I was listening to the noise out in the street. A man went by. I would say from the way he was striking the pavement with his stick that he was either blind or lame. I pitied him. If only he had my mode of transport! My heart was full of thanks and love and I promised myself that I would never do harm to any living thing. With the heat of the fire I fell asleep. But the sleep came over me gradually, and while dozing off, I thought no man alive so happy.

It was night when I awoke.

Chapter Four

It is now the beginning of April. But even so, winter is not yet over. A week ago I had thought that the fine weather was here to stay. But I was wrong. When I awoke this morning, and looked out the window, what did I see but snow!

I didn't get up. To tell you the truth, I am still in bed. I have paper and pencil in my grasp. The wooden leg is on a chair beside me. I am beginning to feel hungry. I haven't eaten much for two days. A small piece of bread, that was all, for I was loath to change my last half-sovereign.

I take hold of it again and begin to hop it on the palm of my hand. I toss it up in the air. I catch it coming down. How hard it is! I put it under the mattress, and pretend that all I have is the penny that's in my pocket.

A penny! The one and only penny that was between me and death! How long would it take a person to die from hunger? I once had nothing to eat for three days, and on the third day I had felt no hunger at all. The pangs of hunger would recede as death was coming closer, until intoxication, then madness, would come over you. And how would death itself come? Like an arrested thief with his back to the wall. If I could wait here quietly until he arrives . . . but those three days, they would be worse than death itself. You would feel so empty inside your gut for the first day, then the dreadful thirst would come, and when you would swallow a mouthful of water to satisfy that awful thirst, you would vomit . . . and after that, you would imagine yourself being pricked by a thousand hot needles.

I get up with a start. I put the half-sovereign into my pocket and, helped by a young man, go slowly, deliberately down the stairs. I get a pennyworth of bread and start to chew it in front of the fire in the big room.

Death from starvation! What a dreadful saying, if properly understood. I could not suffer it . . . but . . . now I have it! I'll go begging, that's what I'll do. I should be good at it if only I could pocket my pride. But wouldn't I have to do it in the end anyway? And wouldn't it be better for me to start now, while I still have the half-sovereign? Wouldn't I be better able to face it? Would it be worth my while? Is there anything else I could take up? Stealing? Yes, that would be better, but I had never practiced it, and it would not be long before you were caught if you had no experience of the trade. What could you hope for then? To go to prison, I suppose. Well, many's the good man was put in prison, and they would feed me there. Sinful? Who said that?

Who invented right and wrong but people with full stomachs? The law of God? When a person is hungry he is not subject to any law. Yes, from now on my trade would be stealing. A better trade than begging for alms, and I should not be long in gaining experience of it. And anything I could not get by cleverness, I could get by force, should I meet a feeble person. I could even fell a strong man with my crutch. What ever made me think that I could die of hunger among all the wealth of this wonderful city?

Snow fell during the night. By now it has turned to slush under the hooves of horses and the feet of men. There is a fog. Heavy fog that would go into your mouth and down your throat; fog that would bring tears to your eyes; fog that would come in the door, and in through the windows, no matter how tightly closed. But the fog is not bothering me. I am looking into the fire, while these thoughts are crowding in on me. I am looking into the fire, and in it I see the great riches I shall get from thievery. . .

Night is coming. I go out. The great city is in hiding under its marvellous cloak of fog. Now and then, you could see the lights of the coaches jumping up in front of you and disappearing with the speed of sparks. A person could be quite close to you and you would not see him until he bumped into you; and before you realised it, he would disappear from sight. But, although the city was hidden, you could hear its noises. Somebody shouting near you. The screech of a distant train. Fog-horns of ships on the river. Thousands of other muffled sounds coming towards you and fading away, all mixed together in one great humming.

I made for the river. I met a sailor. He spoke to me. Would I buy some tobacco from him? I would not, I never smoked."But it's cheap,very cheap, my friend," said the sailor. "Only I need the money so badly, I should not be selling it at all. Here, give me the price of a bed for it. There's a pound weight in it, if there's an ounce."

I shook my head. I was going to leave.

"Maybe you would like this?" he said. "A fine pistol with a silver handle — look, there is a bullet in it. Be careful, my friend! Careful, I say."

"How much?" I asked, in a casual sort of way.

I was satisfied to give him my last half-sovereign for it. I did not know then, while the two of us stood under a lamp beside the river in the City of Darkness, what a poisonous desire I had for the pistol. There was something magical about it. There was something satanic about that silver-handled pistol which forbade me to leave until I had it safe in my trousers pocket.

The sailor was satisfied to sell it to me for a crown piece, because he needed the money so badly. A strange bargain, I thought, as the two of us went to a public house near the river so that I could change my last half-sovereign.

Chapter Five

The young sailor and myself are drinking hard. Neither of us will have much of the money left by the time the night is over, and it does not seem to matter to us. It has been a half-year since I last had a drink, and I can feel the alcohol coursing through my body like a stream of fire, invading every limb. The great sadness and the down-heartedness of this morning in the lodging-house have left me completely. If I can believe myself, there is no great deed which I cannot accomplish.

I started talking, telling marvellous adventure stories to the stout sailor-man beside me, and, of course, all the adventures had been my own. At first I told my tales in English, but before long I changed over to Irish, without realising it.

The public house was full, and everybody there was amazed to hear the strange language, everybody except the sailor. That rogue pretended to understand everything that I was saying. I was very excited, and they all wanted to know what was the matter with me.

A small yellow-faced man who had been sitting in a corner by himself stood up. He was a wrinkled sly-looking little fellow, with two bright eyes sunk deep in his head. You could hardly see them at all under his big black eyebrows. He put a few questions to the sailor. I almost went into fits of laughter when I noticed how his big, long, hooked nose, and his long, pointed, little chin were trying to kiss each other while he was talking. The sailor was happy to tell him my story. He swallowed another large draught of beer and started talking with speed and enthusiasm, while all there were listening carefully.

He told them that I was a German; that I had been a lunatic during one period of my life; that I had killed eight men during that period (some of them drew back from me); that I had been kept in a madhouse for a long time — until the King of that country was satisfied to have me released. My sanity had, of course, returned by this time, and what did I do but go on safari in East Africa, killing lions?

"Exactly," he said, "that is how he came by his dreadful injuries. It was a fierce old lion that came upon him, my friend, while he was asleep. Only that he was asleep, there would have been no danger of that lion finding him, he had always been so careful. But before the poor man could grab spear or firearm, or even scream for help, the King of the Forest sank his claws into the marrow of his bones. Don't you see the marks on him, to this day, my friends?"

He pointed out the scars that the motor car had left on my face. I tried to stop him, but failed. He continued with his story. "But he had a long sharp knife," says he, "and, in the wink of your eye, he had sunk it to the hilt in the heart of the lion. Didn't you, my friend? You certainly did. And didn't you carry the great beast away with you on your back, or as much of him as you could? And was it not I who took you on board the ship, yourself and your burden? And why wouldn't I, my friends, such a strong able man, who had been able to kill the lion and carry him?"

"And what became of his arm and his leg? Alas! It's a sorry tale to tell. The doctor had to amputate them. Such a terrible pity, but there was nothing else for it . . ."

There wasn't a word out of anyone there, but they stared hard at me. Some of them in wonder. Some of them out of pity. More of them too drunk to make anything of the story.

But my jolly sailor was not satisfied with that many lies. He was a fascinating liar, and as fast as he was telling them, he kept on inventing more.

Didn't we both jump ship in Spain, and didn't we walk the length and breadth of that country whilst he put me on exhibition? Didn't hundreds — thousands — come to see me? "When he would tuck his one leg up under him like this (here pushing my leg up under me), and an overcoat around him like this (here taking the little yellow-faced man's overcoat and wrapping it around me) you would not think that he had any legs at all. And, with the way I used to paint his face, and with a great wig of false hair down to his waist, he was a gold mine, a gold mine."

He told the story with such flair, and with such polish, and with his honest face, you could not but like him. All the people there kept crowding in on me so as to get a better look at such an unusual person, but that upset me. I roared at them. They backed away from me. I was delighted that I had succeeded in frightening them. The sailor was having great fun. The little yellow-faced man was as pleased as Punch.

He warned them to keep away from me, that I was dangerous, vicious, and might do them a mischief.

"Keep away from him! Keep away from him, I say!" the sailor and the little man were both shouting.

But there was one woman there who was not frightened. A big woman. A mighty big woman who had a face like a Roman Emperor. Her hair was the colour of the red rowan berry. Her bosom was exposed. There was the smell of drink from her. Her eyes were alight in her head. She sat beside me on the bench. She spoke to me while everybody was looking on.

"You're the queer German," she said, "speaking Irish all night."

I didn't know what was the best thing to say. I felt ashamed in front of her, that I should be in such company, that I should let them have me for a figure of fun.

"It was only a bit of a joke," I said, at last.

"It was no harm. Where do you come from?"

"From Galway."

"From Galway, is it? Do you tell me that?"

"There's no lie in it. But where are you from yourself? You speak Galway Irish."

"I'm from Cill Aodáin."

"From Cill Aodáin! That's not more than twelve miles from Galway City. Wasn't . . . . .born there?" (I named a man who had been one of his country's heroes.)

"That's where he was born," she said; " I went to school with him."

She became pensive. Tears came into her eyes. She dried them with her apron. She drank another mouthful from her glass. We were left by ourselves by this time and the others were not paying any attention to us. Little Yellowface and the sailor were talking to each other in the corner.

"The blackguards," said the Big Red-haired Woman with the face like a Roman Emperor; and not alone had she the face, but she looked as if she would do some dreadful deed, worthy of any Emperor of Rome, if she had the power.

"What blackguards?" said I, to placate her, for she was in a rage.

"Don't you know who I mean? Aren't you an Irishman?"

She was in such a rage of bad temper, and in such a fit of anger, that I could hardly understand what she was saying.

"They hung our priests, they plundered our people, they exiled our monks and our friars, they laid waste to our country."

"That's true." I said.

"They put Wolfe Tone in prison," said she, "they put Emmet in prison, they put . . . in prison (Here she mentioned the hero she had spoken of earlier). They put me in prison . . . they put . . ."

With that she put a stop to herself.

"And you tried to strike a blow for your country too?" I asked.

"I tried, darling. . . but it wasn't for that I was put in prison."

"For what, then?"

"Drink," said the Big Red-haired Woman.

The two of us remained silent for a good while — she full of rage on account of all that she — and her country, had suffered, I thinking about our unhappy predicament.

The rest of the company was full of merriment and of loud-voiced high spirits. The whole place was bright and glittering under the little electric bulbs which were of every colour in the rainbow. Music playing — and not alone did the music machine play of its own accord, but it showed a variety of pictures as well; the lovely waterfall, the swift flowing river, the great forest with the moon shining above the trees, the sea and a sinking ship. But the two exiles sitting together on the bench paid little attention to the music or the pictures or the conviviality; they were sad and depressed, with the tragedy of life in their hearts.

The Big Red-haired Woman jumped up suddenly. She put her two arms around me and began to kiss me in front of everyone.

Chapter Six

When Yellowman and the sailor had finished their conversation they came over to me. Little Yellowmansat down on the bench beside me. He seemed to be very happy with himself and with the world.

"Would you come along with me?" he asked me.

"Where would I be going?" said I.

"Do you not recognise who I am?"

"Who are you?"

He told me. He was a showman who travelled the country. He had a circus which comprised many wonders and horrors, wild beasts and other attractions. He spent most of his time in Ireland but used to visit London to hire acts for his circus. If he found the right people, he would pay them well.

"How much would you pay me?" I asked.

"Fifty shillings a week," and he looked at me sharply.

I thought it a huge sum of money, but I didn't tell him that.

"Three pounds." I said.

He began to tell me that all I would have to do was to double up my good leg under me so that it would not be seen; wear a wig of long black hair; paint my cheeks with fearsome colours, and put up some howls from time to time so as to terrify the public when they came to see me.

"Three pounds," I said again.

"It's a bargain," said he, and gave me some money.

I promised to meet him at ten o'clock the following morning; he said good-bye, and off he went.

I did not stay long after he left. I made my farewells to the Big Red-haired Woman, and moved off in the little wheelchair I had been given in the lodging-house.

The fog was dreadful. A fog like it has never been seen in the city before or since. People would not find it easy to make their way home.

I thought at first, as I was moving along in the little chair, that it had been a great blessing from God to meet the showman. I should not be obliged to go stealing as I had planned before I left the house. I was no longer in danger from hunger and want. I had an income of three pounds a week. Three pounds a week! It was big money. How pleased I was!

But a great sadness came over my heart. It was coming over me gradually. I could not get rid of it. Had I not sold myself for three pounds a week? Had I not turned myself into a wonder, a horror, a public spectacle. If my friends and relations should know about it, how they would despise me! That a man of my surname would do a thing like this — making himself a figure of fun in public, and that he should be doing it for money!

What would they say in Galway? That was the question I put to myself, as many a poor exile had done before me, far away from his home town. I despised myself. I was fed up with myself. Then the shame vanished. Anger took its place. It maddened me. I was out of my mind. I began to drive my wheelchair on purpose at the passers-by on the footpath. I kept telling them that they were were trying to knock me over — myself and my little wheelchair. And when they would begin to apologise, I would start to curse and swear at them. I took great pleasure in this. Was I not now a public spectacle, and should such a person not be entitled to say anything he likes?

A man was passing by — a man in a posh suit — and I asked him for a match. He was giving it to me when I put up a great roar (I had the idea of practising the roar that Little Yellowmanwanted) and I shouted — "Don't you see that I am a horror! A horror! A public spectacle!" But he was gone like the wind. I burst into peals of laughter, and could not stop until the tears were in my eyes. What fun it was to see the posh person going off at a gallop. I suppose he thought I was really a madman. A lunatic! But he was wrong. Hadn't I only told him I was a horror and a public spectacle ? . . .

There is a big wide road beside the river at the place where I am now. There are fine large houses on the North side of it. The river is on the South side. There are seats here and there along by the river. Fine green trees on both sides. Wandering people often spend the night on these seats. There were three men on the first seat this foggy night. They were asleep when I came upon them. I put up a roar — Yellowman's roar — and they jerked up in an instant. If you could only have seen the fear in their eyes. I said my piece. "Don't you see that I am a horror — a horror and a public spectacle?" They would have run off only I said, "A cup of coffee and a piece of bread — I need them badly now. Would you like a cup, friends?"

"In God's name don't be mocking us," said one of them.

"I am not mocking. But if you do not want it, then don't come with me."

They followed me. Why should I not spend the money? Wouldn't I have too much of it from now on? Three pounds a week! I should not have half that much only that I lost the use of my limbs. Is it not well for me that I am a horror and a public spectacle. A public spectacle — I liked the name a lot. A public spectacle! A public spectacle! I started to say the words over and over again, like a child playing a game.

But why should I not spend the money? I told every wretch I met to follow me and drink a cup of coffee with me. I had forty followers by the time we reached the coffee stall.

They were thin and ragged. Some of them, when they saw the food, had a look in their eyes like the look in the eyes of a tiger. They were famished with the cold and the hunger. They wolfed the food whilst the sweat poured off them from the heat of the coffee and from the effort they had to put into drinking it. Some of them had not eaten for so long that they were unable to keep down the food . . . I caught sight of myself in a tall mirror that had an advertisement for cigarettes.

"You lot look horrible, and hideous and dangerous," I said, "from the lack and the need of money: I am a horror, but I am getting money for it." I was becoming quite eloquent when the Big Woman who looked like a Roman Emperor caught hold of me.

"Are you not gone home yet?" said she. "I had no right to let you go off like that, no right at all. And I would not have, either, if I had thought you would be spending your money like this — on people like this."

She looked fiercely at me. It seemed that some of the crowd were afraid of her, that they knew who she was. They edged away from her. Some went off.

"And, as for you, Michael," she said, "I thought you had sense. I thought that. You have too, only for the drink. And I say this from my own experience. You won't be able to go home now. The road is long. The fog is dreadful. And you are almost drunk . . . you will have to come home with me tonight. You can have a blanket beside the fire until morning. You'll be comfortable there. Let us go in the name of God. Isn't it a dreadful night? May God preserve us! Don't mind the wheel, Michael, I'll push you. That's the way!"

She pushed the little wheelchair before her. You would think I was a child, and she my mother.

Chapter Seven

We arrived at the home of the Big Red-haired Woman. She had a large empty room at the top of a house. At first it seemed to be altogether empty, but it was not. There was a bed there, a kind of a bed; a long bench against the wall, but there was no sign of a table, or any crockery or cooking utensils.

There is no light in the big room, only the light from the fire, but that is enough for us. We are sitting together in front of it, talking over all we have seen of life, all that has happened to each of us since we arrived in this foreign country. And it was many the story the Big Red-haired Woman had to tell, although they were not fairy tales or tales of heroic fiction, but stories of horror, grief and shame.

Now and again, she takes hold of my hand, and begins to fondle it with kindness and affection, as my mother used to do long ago, when I was a small child. The anger that was in me out on the street, while I was going astray in the fog, has disappeared. There is not a trace of it left. I am as quiet, as gentle, as trusting, as affectionate as a little baby. The Big Red-haired Woman lays a hand on my cheek — on that cheek that is ruined with scars. Its hideousness does not repel her. It would seem that her affection for me is all the stronger because of it — and by the light of the fire I can see that she has great pity for me. The kind of pity my mother would have for me if she could see me now. I lean my head back on her shoulder, my eyes closed. I had felt, for one tiny second, that this was indeed my mother, and that I was a child once again . . .

The fire has almost gone out. I am no longer on the bench, but am lying on the floor, wrapped in an old blanket from the Red-haired Woman's Bed. She is sitting beside me on the floor, trying to banish the heavy depression which has been coming over me again. She does not like to see me sad. She would prefer my anger to that. She begins to sing softly :

" Like this I put my baby to sleep, in a cradle of gold on a floor of peace, or . . ."

She is unable to finish the rest of the verse, but that doesn't upset her. She put a few nonsensical words together, that went with the rhyme, and finished it with :

". . . to be rocked in the breeze."

She sang the same verse over and over again until I was almost asleep. She must have thought I was fast asleep, for she got up quickly, and threw herself on the bed.

All she had wanted to do was to put me to sleep with the lullaby.

I awoke. There was still a little light coming from the fire. The fog was seeping in through the window, and through the door, and down the chimney. The great city was asleep, although you could hear a noise now and again, even if you could not tell from what direction it was coming, only that it seemed to come from very far away — from a thousand miles away, you might think.

The Big Red-haired Woman was not asleep. Her face was turned to the wall, and she was weeping bitterly. Sometimes, it seemed not to be weeping, really, but rather as if there was a heavy load on her heart, which she was straining to throw off. She would be very quiet for about two minutes, and then would let out a great sigh, and from every sigh you would think that the load on her heart was rising and falling in her throat. I should have gone over to comfort her if I had not thought that the crying was doing her good. I had seen women weeping before and it had done them a lot of good.

She eventually took hold of herself. She was probably feeling sleepy. I was dozing off myself when I noticed that there was a light in the room beneath us. There was nothing between the two levels but the boards, and the light was coming up through the chinks. It was a stable beneath us, and the noise of the horses being brought in after their night's work kept me awake almost until morning.

In the morning, you would not have thought by the Big Red-haired Woman that she had ever cried. She was as merry as the lark in the clear air, and as light-footed as a stonechat whilst she got the breakfast. I was half awake, half asleep, when I heard her singing, while she worked away.

It was past ten o'clock when we finished eating. We went out to have our last drink together. There was a crowd of women in the public house, and, of course, they all knew the Red-haired Woman well. We had not been long there when she went out. She had forgotten something in her room.

The women began to talk about her. She was well known in the neighbourhood. Had she not saved three people from drowning in the river? And had she not received great praise for that? And a testimonial from an organisation which took an interest in that kind of work? She certainly had — except that the testimonial — a gold medal — had been sold long ago, and the money spent on drink. Big Maggie, as they called her, had only that one fault. And another night, when a mad horse was galloping through the street, did she not catch it, and would have held on to it too, only that she broke her leg? And the night she was drunk and knocked down a policeman! They really knocked fun out of that adventure. Did she not sit on his chest, and for pure mischief, take his whistle out of his tunic and blow it?

She came in then, which put an end to the conversation.

It was time for me to go. Little Yellowman would be waiting for me. I bade farewell, with a blessing, to the Big Red-haired Woman, and hurried off. But I have often thought of her since. Indeed I have often thought of visiting that Big Red-haired Woman who had the face of a Roman Emperor. And I was fated to see her again.

Little Yellowman was waiting for me in the other public house.

Chapter Eight

We are travelling Ireland at present — myself and little Yellowman, and his horrors, and wonders and wild beasts. We have traversed the province of Munster, every town in it, from Waterford to Limerick. Last night we arrived in Galway, the city where I was born.

We have a parade in every town, on our first day there, to let the people know of the coming of Little Yellowman and his travelling circus. I am always in the parade. I am in it today on the streets of Galway. I am sitting up in a chariot. There is a brass chain around my neck, fastened to the floor of the chariot. Another chain around my waist. Long black hair falling down around my shoulders. The hair tossed in great tresses so that it hides my face when I shake myself. But my face is so well painted that I am not permitted to hide it. I shake my head again so as to put the hair in order, and, when I do, the great brass chains make a loud clanging. Then I have to put up a great roar — the roar I gave on that night when I was going astray in the fog. Then my keepers (by whom I am surrounded all the time) start to lash me with their long stiff whips. The people draw back from them in fear. But if they only knew it! The roar and the chains and the long stiff whips are only part of little Yellowman's trickery, so as to draw in the crowd in the evening . . .

And that is how I first paraded the streets of Galway, having been away for so many years. How strangely things happen!

I see many people I know on the streets. They do not

recognise me. How could they with the state I am in? Had I the least fear that they might, shame would not have allowed me to come . . . I pass by the house I was born in. Who lives in it now? Does it matter? I shall never live there again. The way we are taking now is the way I used to take to school long ago. Old memories start crowding in on me while I am putting on this show for the people of my home town. I feel nostalgic and lonely to be here when nobody recognises me. But I can recognise many of the people around me. What a surprise for Martin Smith over there if I called out to him! The poor simple man would think I had witchcraft if I were to shout: "Who stole Nora O'Malley's gander?"

"Martin! Martin!" I shouted at the top of my voice, "who stole the gander?"

Everyone there burst out laughing, and mocking poor Martin. Little Yellowman was delighted. They would all be sure to come in to him in the evening. What money he would make! A smile broadened across his face, and he started to wash his hands in air, he was so happy . . .

But I shall kill that thieving little yellow sprat one of these days. How he makes me hate him! How was I so misguided as to sell my body to him for three pounds a week? How was I so unfortunate as to make myself into a horror and a spectacle?

For the money, was it? Don't say it. Who could compete with me in the spending of money when I had it? (Why is a person always so slow to say to himself that he once nearly died of hunger? And yet he will say it to others). It was Little Yellowman who tempted me with his money. Wasn't he the villain? I tell you, little Yellowman, here is the one who could cheerfully choke you, be you devil or angel!

Imagine my delight to see the grey-blue colour coming over your dirty yellow face! How my heart would leap while I examined the black marks left by my fingers on your skinny neck. What a jig of joy I would dance to see the eyes bulging out of your head like two hens' eggs, getting bigger, bigger, all the time . . . ?

At this moment he came along himself. When he saw how agitated I was he was more than pleased. He thought I was making a great effort to put fear and terror into the hearts of the people so that more of them would come to the circus in the evening. I was a great fellow. He had decided to give me the four pounds a week I had been asking for that morning. I was worth more. He looked at me, and started to wink his eye so that I would understand he was happy to give it to me. He stuck up four fingers. He winked again. I was getting angry. Why was he teasing me like that? Wasn't I making his fortune? Who would come to his circus without me? Where would they be going?

I made a mighty feint. It gave me great heart to feel how strong the muscles were in my good arm. The chain began to chime like the little brass bells you often see hanging from beneath a horse's neck. I gave a roar, a tremendous roar of anger, but the roar was directed at little Yellowman. When I gave this roar, he looked at me sharply, for it was not the roar I usually practiced. He hadn't thought I would be capable of a roar like that. But when he saw the anger and the hatred and the evil following on each other's heels in my eyes and on my painted cheeks, there wasn't a man in Galway happier than he. He began to wash his hands in the air, with a smile on his face.

That was a mannerism he had, when he was very contented in his mind.

I remembered the pistol I had bought from the sailor that night long ago. It was still in my trousers' pocket. Should I shoot him? Had I the courage to put a bullet through his heart? Oh, if I were anywhere else but in Galway, where I should be recognised before I were hanged, you would not be long for this world, little mister Yellowman.

He looked at me again. All I did was put out my tongue at him and I made a nasty noise with my mouth. He began to laugh. Everybody on the street began to laugh. You could hear every peal of their laughter a mile away.

I heard every single snigger. I heard Little Yellowman warning the crowd to keep away from me, that I was out of my mind, but "come along tonight," he was shouting, "come along to see him tonight — only two pence each. He is the terror of the world.

. . . The terror of the world — come along tonight and hear all about his strange and horrible deeds. Come tonight! Two pence each, that's all! Two pence only to see the great monstrosity — to speak to him, to touch him, two pence each!"

I had my eyes closed. Oblivious of everything. But the voice of Little Yellowman and the shouting of the crowd were making unpleasant music in my ears, in spite of me. Until that day, I had never thought it might be a great blessing from God to be deaf.

Chapter Nine

When we returned to the field where little Yellowman's circus was being held, I went into my booth to rest myself, and to collect my thoughts.

I took off the black wig, the great brass chains and the multi-coloured coat I had to wear during the parade. I picked up a little book of songs and started to read it. But I didn't read many of the songs. Little Yellowman's people were making so much noise that I could not keep my eyes on the book. Some of them were looking after the wild animals; some driving stakes into the ground and erecting the canvas booths; others setting up the swing boats; two or three at one side preparing food; a young woman mounted on the back of a white horse dressed like the fairy queen in the stories; a tall young man with a whip in his hand running behind the horse; his hair dyed beautifully and a tall cornered cap on his head; only for the cap and the hair-dye, you would not think he had anything to do with the circus, since he had not yet put on his fancy uniform; Little Yellowman completely at ease up on a shimmering golden chariot, supervising all the work. Every one of them cursing and complaining and swearing, all except myself who was trying to read my book. Yes, myself — and the Fat Lady.

I saw her coming towards me; here she was, sailing across the field, carrying a big dish. She moved like a great ship swaying across the ocean. She seemed every minute as if she were about to spill everything from the dish, but she didn't.

She stood in the doorway, and if I had really been in the mood for reading, I still could not have read a word, as her huge bulk blocked out the sunlight.

She was another one of little Yellowman's public spectacles. Originally she had not been altogether so fat; you would often see fatter women who did not take part in any show. But she was short in stature, and had an enormous head, with broad shoulders, great obese arms and heavy buttocks! And every day she was growing fatter and fatter, since she had nothing to do but eat and drink her fill. Anybody who saw the rich tasty food and the strong nourishing drinks she got from Little Yellowman would have to praise his altruism and generosity.

And hadn't she a pitiful greed for rich food and sweet drinks? And wasn't it she who could sleep for twelve hours of the clock? She was lazy and lethargic by nature. She was heavy, slow, sluggish and easygoing. There was nothing she liked more than to eat and drink her fill and to throw herself down on the long grass on a summer's day to sunbathe. She would remain like that all the long day from dawn to dark without moving except when she was guzzling the food.

It was no wonder that she was getting fatter day by day. It was no wonder that Little Yellowman was so happy in his mind. No wonder he washed his hands in the air every time he looked at her.

And she never asked him for a penny. She was happy with her keep. And when you would see her dressed up for show, (dressed so as to make her appear much fatter than she was) you would say that Little Yellowman should be more than pleased with his handiwork.

She came into the middle of the booth.

"See what I have for you," said she, showing me the big dish. "A scrap of chicken, a scrap of fat bacon, white cabbage, floury potatoes, and gravy."

When she had said the word 'gravy' she stopped. She

almost closed her eyes, and pursed her lips as though she would love to have been swallowing it. If anybody ever showed delight in the face, she was showing it now.

"A scrap of fat bacon!" said I. There was at least a pound in it.

"Take it," she said, "you must be hungry."

She laid the dish on the ground beside me. She sat on the other side of it.

"I'll eat a bit of the chicken myself," she said, and started eating greedily.

She seemed to be slightly ashamed to be eating so much, since I had eaten so little.

"Why aren't you eating it?" she asked, with a big fat piece in her mouth and the gravy dripping down on her blouse.

"Because I'm not hungry," I said.

"Reach behind you," she said. "There it is."

I did so. There was a large can of beer behind me. I drank a mouthful of it, and passed it over to her.

"Don't you take a great interest in reading?" said the Fat Lady, taking up the little song book that I had left aside when she came in.

She started to read the song I had been reading myself when she came in.

"Rise up, Willie Reilly," said she, having first swallowed the food in her mouth.

"Rise up, Willie Reilly, and come along with me,
I'm going to quit my father's house, and quit this countiree,
To leave my father's houses, his dwellings, and free lands,
And go along with Reilly, as you may understand."

"Oh! Isn't it lovely," said she, having read that much, but

I wasn't sure if it was the song which was lovely or the piece of chicken she put into her mouth after she had finished reading.

Little Yellowman's people were still working under pressure. Cursing and swearing. The young woman who was dressed as a fairy queen was on the back of the white horse, practising jumping through a golden hoop, as the horse circled the ring. But the wild beasts had stopped bellowing. Their bellies were full.

"It is time for you to go now," I said to the Fat Lady.

"Am I not time enough?" said she, pressing in on me.

"I shall feel happier and more contented here," she said, and laid her head on my chest.

Chapter Ten

O nly for the fact that Little Yellowman himself came to dress me up and to prepare me for the night, she would probably not have gone at all.

The black wig was put back on my head. The brass chains were put around my neck and waist. (My cheeks had already been painted). My leg was tucked back in under me. The multi-coloured greatcoat was put around me. The torch above me was lit, and what with it swinging in the wind, and with the shadows coming and going over my face, you would think me more hideous than I really was.

The gates were opened, and the people started coming in. They were mostly teenagers. And what a happy lot! So full of fun! So full of interest in everything! Little Yellowman can't control them. His helpers can't control them. They are not for controlling. Some of them trying to catch sight of me through the chinks between the boards of the booth. Another lot reading the notice above the door. They are reading the notice slowly and deliberately, like people who had not much experience of reading. I can hear every word :

GEORGE COFF
TWO PENCE

The madman, missing one arm and two legs. Look at his hair. It has not been cut for two years. And look at the hatred in his eyes! He murdered eight men in Germany. See the big long knife that did the deed and see the traces of blood on it still.

"Two pence! Oh, if I had another halfpenny I could go in," said one young fellow.

"I'll give you a penny for your old black knife, Marcus."

"You were going to give me a penny-halfpenny for it yesterday," says Marcus.

" I was . . . but. . . . but I want to see the madman . . ."

"Give me the penny-halfpenny," says Marcus, who had the black knife in his fist and was teasing the other lad with it. The latter was between two minds. He coveted the knife greatly, but if he parted with his money, he wouldn't get to see me . . .

"Give me the penny-halfpenny," says Marcus," . . . and I'll tell you all about him when I come out."

He got the money.

Two more came in.

And two more. And they were coming and going until a good part of the night was over. Every word that came out of their mouths I took as an insult. But, of course, they did not think I understood their speech. Even so, they made me hate them. In any other place, their talk would not have bothered me. But here in Galway, where I was born! Imagine if they knew who I was! If they knew that it was one of their own people who was being exhibited to them as a terrifying freak!

Anger took hold of me. Madness and rage and hatred took hold of me. What could I do to really strike terror into them? I could not think of anything I could do. Why should they be coming to look at me anyway? Was I not a man? Had I not feeling and intelligence and understanding like every man? Are they Christians? Is that lovely young woman over there who is looking at me now a Christian? And she does not pity me. I can see it in her eyes that she is amazed and frightened that somebody like me can exist at all. She shivers when she sees the blood-stained knife. But wait. I shall give you a real fright, lovely young woman.

"Oh, Michael," said she to the young man who was with her, "Oh, Michael, tell Mary to come in; she will never see a sight like this again."

"She is a little frightened, you know how timid she is . . .," said he, but I paid no attention to him.

"Mary! Mary! Come here till you see him," said the young woman, going to the door of the booth, without taking any notice of what her companion was saying to her. " You have never seen such a sight before."

Mary came in, but I paid no attention to her. I had my two eyes closed, while I was speculating as to the best way to really scare them. The woman who had come in first had the blood-stained knife in her hand, and was asking the other woman to hold it. When she went to do that, (I did not know she was going to do it as my eyes were closed), I put a fierce expression on my face, and put up two terrible roars, as a bull might when he feels the knife at his throat, and I started to twist my body as if I were an eel in a man's fist. The knife fell from her hand. She nearly went into a faint. Only for the man who was with her — I found out afterwards it was her husband — only for him, she would have been a heap on the floor of the booth.

I was delighted that I had frightened them. Only for the fact that the first woman who came in was so shapely, so beautiful, so well-dressed, I should not have bothered with them. Were they not uncultivated people who would come to look at a person like me? I'll warrant you they will not come again! This trip will be enough for them.

The woman who had been fainting was being brought out for air.

"Michael, Michael," said she, pitifully, "why did you bring me here?" I opened my eyes suddenly when I heard the voice.

How well I recognised the woman who owned that voice!

I was on the point of calling her over and telling her who I was when Little Yellowman himself came in. You never saw a man so overjoyed. He had heard those two roars I had given, from the other side of the field.

"Wasn't it the lucky day I first met you!" said he, washing his hands in air. "I f you will give two roars like those, three times every night, I shall give you five pounds a week."

He was talking to himself as he went out, and saying that all the people wanted was to be well frightened and they would come in their droves to see the madman.

But I took no notice of what he had said. I wasn't thinking about the circus at all. My mind was on the young woman who had been brought out. On Mary Lee, my own first cousin, and not without reason.

Not without reason, I say, for I was once engaged to her. Oh, Mary, if you had only known that it was Michael Mullen who was before you tonight in the guise of a madman! But for you, I should never have left home in the first instance. But for you I should not be in the shameful condition that I am in today. It is you who are responsible for every misfortune that came in my direction, Mary, if you only knew it. Neither myself nor my family had much wealth. My mother and five brothers had only one small holding between us, and, of course, Mary, you would not have been willing to marry me until I had first earned some money in England. Don't you remember that night when I bade you farewell, Mary? Little did either of us expect that we should meet again in this way. And how many hours did I not spend thinking about you until I heard that you had married your second cousin, Michael Kierans? And that was Michael Kierans who was with you. Did you recognise me, Mary? Had you the slightest idea who it was? If you had, what would you have said? You would have had pity for me, wouldn't you? You would have tried to get me out of the clutches of Little Yellowman, would you not? But I do not want pity. I don't want a place to live, either. I really don't know what I want. I never knew. And aren't there many more in the same predicament?

. . . Little Yellowman came by. He was not too pleased that I was not roaring.

The booth was full to overflowing. Everybody there expecting me to pull some stunt that would terrify his neighbour. Noise and bustle out in the field. Steam-engines making music, and screeching occasionally. Peals of laughter from a crowd here. Angry threatening shouts from a crowd over there.

But I did not notice anything that was going on. My appearance could only be compared to that of the Fat Lady when she had eaten and drunk her fill. My head leaning backwards. My eyes half-closed. I was as motionless as the pole in the ground behind me.

But if I looked peaceful and contented, there was neither peace nor content in my heart. Since Mary and her husband departed I was left without any courage. The rage and hatred and anger that had overwhelmed me during the day, after I reached my home town, had left me. But they had left me agitated. Very much so. Agitated like the sea after a great storm. But I did not believe I was the victim of an evil destiny. All that had happened to me had been my own fault. Why had I not the providence to marry her, even though we had little of the world's goods? If I had, I should still have the use of my limbs, a wife, and with God's will, a family of sons and daughters growing up around me . . .

This last thought that came to me, cut me to the quick. And, as was usual with me, when I started to meditate on the blessings which had never come in my direction, I could see them clearly, in front of my mind's eye, in brightly coloured pictures, coming and going incessantly.

I paid no attention to little Yellowman, who kept

pestering me to let out another screech; I paid no attention to the tumult out in the field; I paid no attention to the people of Galway who were coming in crowds to inspect me. It was these many-coloured pictures, and they only, that preoccupied me.

In the first picture, there was a cozy little house on the edge of a branchy wood; a little stream meandering through the wood, and throwing itself down the rocks to the south-west of it; the wood itself full of flowers; the sweet perfume of the whitethorn and the chestnut and the pine tree in my nostrils; night falling; myself making my way home through the wood; heavy and tired and weary after the day's work; a lamp hanging on the wall of the house to steer me home; a woman moving to and fro about the house although I can only see her as she passes door or window.

I go in. Crossing the threshold, I hear the soft sweet voices of the children. I kiss Pat and little Brigid and they run to tell their mother that I am home. The mother comes — any wonder that it is Mary I see, with Colm on her shoulder? But it is hard to please him. He has been expecting apples. Didn't I promise them to him this morning?

. . . But time passed. The new year came. Colm was now able to walk by himself. Wearing little knee-breeches. Curly black hair falling down around his shoulders; He follows me through the wood, his voice making music for me . . .

But it is only a false vision. I have neither wife nor child, nor house nor land, I have nothing of the sort. All I have are my thoughts; sad, shameful thoughts, thinking on that part of my life that is spent: thoughts of hope and joy, imagining how things might have been for me if — yes, if I had been another person.

The people are gone. The whole circus is asleep. Little Yellowman himself is asleep. May it be a sleep without wakening, you blackguard! All I can hear from my booth is the sound of one of little Yellowman's wild beasts, moving to and fro in his prison. To and fro, to and fro without relief, as if he were remembering all that he had left behind him in his native country — and the blessings that had not come his way . . . or maybe he only has a sick stomach after all the food he has eaten.

Half an hour passed. An hour. Two hours. Three hours. Sleep was not coming, as I tossed from side to side. Betimes, wondering whether it was his digestion or his old memories that tormented the wild beast who could not find rest in his cage. Betimes thinking of the uproar there would be if I were to set him free.

In the end, there was nothing for it but get up and go out in the fresh air.

Chapter Eleven

Was there ever before such a night as this? How close and warm it is. Nobody should stay in bed on a night like it. The devils! (If they don't wash these blankets, there'll be trouble. I swear it !) A sheet and a blanket will do me . . .

I wrap the sheet around me and lie on the dry ground under a bush at the edge of the field. I take no notice of the different calls of the wild beasts locked up nearby. I look across the bay at the ancient rocky hills of the Burren. They are blue. The sky is blue. But look at the difference between the two blues. You would think that the hills were gathering to themselves all the black pigment in the blue of the sky. That it was pouring straight down on them as if it was heavier than the air. And the sea is a different colour from either of them, although you would have to call it blue, too. There is the same difference between the blue of the sea and the blue of the hills as there is between a person's moods, depending on whether he is calm and easy, or full of rage. The sea is not angry or raging tonight — it is very calm — but it has an angry colour. I close both my eyes, and try to combine those three blues in one — in one single shade of blue. And it seems to me that no eye has ever seen such a lovely colour as this . . .

I have just said to myself that the sea had an angry colour: I have always thought that there is a close connection between colour and the emotions that come over the human heart. As if you were to say, that hatred has a colour, that love has a colour, and that dread has a colour of its own. There are many mysteries that might be solved, and many knots that could be unravelled if a deep study were made of the properties of colour.

And, gazing at the sky, and at the sea, and at the old stony hills of the Burren, it came into my mind that colours are closely related, not alone to the moods of the human being, but also to the sounds we hear. That music and colour are related. That every note has its colour, if it could be seen.

But what is the matter with me to be having these thoughts in the middle of the night while little Yellowman's wild beasts are roaring like demons close by? I can't help it. I could not live at all if I spent all my time brooding on my own misfortunes. And strange! I have only just remembered that it was in this very field that I won the prize for running long ago. And wasn't it I who had the turn of speed! My poor father, may he rest in peace, thought that there wasn't a youngster in Ireland who could out-run me. Maybe there wasn't on that day. But today? Anyway, if I had been reminiscing over things like that, I should not have been able to spend such a relaxing night.

Is it dawn? There is not a sound to be heard. Even the wild beasts are asleep. There is a whitening coming into the eastern sky. That whitening is spreading itself across the whole sky, like a small drop of milk poured into a glass of water.

The white is trying to master the blue. They are locked in combat, and the light is steadily overcoming the darkness. Imperceptibly, the hills, and the sea, and the trees beside me are changing colour. It is in the eastern sky that the most light is being created. The stars are being quenched. I can now see only the brightest of them. Were they not beautiful poetic names, those names that I gave them last night when I could not think of their classical names? Now even the brightest ones are disappearing. There is magnificent work going on in the eastern firmament. That end of the sky which was blue a little while ago is now blue and red and purple, except that the colours are separating themselves from each other. The red is now below. The purple is above it but you cannot tell for certain where the purple begins and the red finishes. The blue is above that again, vaulted above us as far as the western horizon, and the white getting the better of it minute by minute.

What's that? A lark, invisible on high. But she pours down a stream of music as sweet as ever was heard by human ear. Who was the idiot who said that this celestial musician does not know that she sings? That it is only as if she were clearing her throat for the day? Rubbish! Let him keep his opinion. I shall not gainsay him. Am I listening to the music at all? I don't think so. I am not listening to it, rather it is seeping through every fibre of my being, like water poured on sugar. I forget all about the varying colours of the sky, and the hills, and the sea, until the lark has vanished with her song.

I am sitting beside a hedgerow, and there are great things going on in the hedgerow too. The little creatures of the countryside are awake. They are starting to ready themselves for the work of a new day. And how they are humming. Humming and whispering. A green insect with eight legs comes out of the hedge, but departs quickly. Maybe I frightened him, or maybe he doesn't like the dew. Something dropped onto the back of my head. It was a kind of snail, and when I flicked him away, it seemed as though he were beseeching me not to kill him, as he lay on the ground, belly up. I let him go, and he slithered slowly out of sight.

The whispering of little creatures still goes on. The combat of the colours is being waged in the sky. What seem like golden rays are extending upwards from the eastern horizon. The rays are turning that end of the sky into a lake of gold. The top of a golden ball is rising up above the Earth.

Rising, rising, rising, and gilding mountain, hill and plain; bay, inlet and island — and even little Yellowman's circus.

The King of the Day has arrived.

Yes, and the Fat Lady. Here she is, with a look of delight on her plump face.

"Oh, I have found you at last, dear," was the first thing she said, "I was very worried when I didn't find you in the booth." She flopped down beside me.

What is up with her that she will not leave me be? Why won't she leave me to my thoughts?

Why must she keep on following me around from place to place as if she were a puppy dog? Haven't I often called her by the first cruel name that came to my tongue? How much more often have I beaten her to try and keep her away from me? But it never did me any good. She would only laugh! And that laugh! It was her laugh that really got me down. It used to leave its impression on her bloated face for fully half an hour. As bad as I was, I almost used to start laughing myself to see her at it.

And when I beat her, she would only come back to me as friendly as ever, begging for forgiveness, like a dog that had been chastised. I was finding it totally impossible to keep her away from me.

"What brought you here?" I asked, angrily.

She looked at me lovingly.

"Be off with you," I said, "or . . . . . "

She looked lovingly at me again. There were tears in her eyes, but there was still a smile on her lips.

"Be off," I said fiercely.

The smile disappeared. Then the tears came in earnest, although she was trying to keep them back. "Michael! Michael!" she pleaded, the tears flowing down her cheeks. She put her hand into her bosom, drew out a little bottle of whiskey, and offered it to me. I was, of course, loath to accept it from her, although I was feeling a bit of a chill after the night . . . Even so, I threw the bottle on the ground the moment I laid hand on it. It was warm from the heat of her body. It disgusted me. "Be off with you," I said, brandishing my crutch, and threatening her with it.

She didn't believe I was in earnest. She didn't believe I would hit her with it. But I would have, only that she put her two strong formidable arms around me. She began to hug me and kiss me until suddenly Little Yellowman appeared beside us, with a loud sneeze. She ran off. Little Yellowman didn't stay either, but I would swear that he was singing a love song as he hurried away.

As God is my judge, I shall kill that little villain as soon as I get the chance . . . but the big Fat Lady . . . Is there another woman in the world who would not find my condition obnoxious only she? For fear of becoming attracted to her, I shall have to . . . Alas! I must not say it.

Chapter Twelve

It was not long before I got my chance with little Yellowman. That evening who but he should come into my booth. He looked as if he had something on his mind, as if he were anxious about something.

" I should like," he said, "to have a quiet sensible conversation with you."

"The four pounds a week you promised . . ."

"No," said he, interrupting me, " but a much more important subject."

"Let us have it, then," said I, "and let me get on with my reading."

"Young man," he said, with anger in his voice, "young man," he said, "don't you be so foolish as to think you can do what you like around here, or it will be the worse for you. I have met people like you before — met them before you were born, and they didn't do themselves much good. They didn't stay with me very long, and were none too happy when they left. "

He said all this very quickly, in a very excited manner, but I couldn't be sure that he was in earnest, or if he was only pretending to be angry. But I didn't mind which. I couldn't guess, either, what was on his mind, and I didn't care. Standing there under the lamp, with the light falling on his wrinkled yellow face, he would have made anybody laugh. He made me feel like laughing, anyway. I would knock some fun out of him. And I did.

He started off again.

"Young man," he said, — he never called anybody

anything else when he was angry, no matter what age they were, "don't you imagine, young man, that you can get away with everything here. Because you can't. I saw you this morning — and others saw you . . . "

" But surely you must know," said I, and was going to tell him the truth of the matter, when he interrupted me. And I knew what was in his mind.

"When my poor father was dying, twenty years ago (may God rest his soul)," said he, "he gave me this piece of advice. 'The Trott family have been on the road now for fifty years,' he said, 'and no evil deed or bad conduct was ever tolerated in their circus. Make sure it will always be so.' 'I will, father, I will', I said, 'as long as I live.' 'May you have luck, then, son,' said he, 'God will reward you', and he slipped away like a trout. And from that day forward, I have kept up the reputation of my family. I have never acted as master over my people, especially over the women, but have always been, as it were, in *loco parentis*, and if my father is in Heaven tonight, looking down at his beloved son, he will bear witness . . . "

From the way he was saying the words, so full of emotion and sincerity, it seemed to me that he was really in earnest, that he really thought I had been trying to seduce the Fat Lady. But I only understood half of the story and I never knew it all until many years later. I thought, at first, to tell him my side of it, but some devil of mischief took hold of me. I was trying to think up some kind of prank, and if I should succeed, there would be fun.

"I shall have to let you go, young man," said he, "even though that is the only fault I have to find with you." "Well," I said, "if I have to go, can't I bring her with me?"

"Bring her with you?" said he, and I thought he was going to hit me. "Bring her with you! Bring her with you! My soul to the devil, and be damned! The man must be really mad!"

"I am not mad," I said solemnly. "I am engaged to be married."

"Engaged!"

He nearly fell into a weakness. I had to say something, or I would have burst out laughing. "Engaged!" he said, again.

"Engaged," said I. "Do you not believe me?"

He looked at me. We looked at each other.

"Ask her yourself, if you don't believe me," said I.

One of his people was passing by the door of the booth.

"Tell Nelly to come over here," he said to him, "Tell her I want her." (Nelly was what they called the Fat Lady).

The Fat Lady came in, frightened out of her wits. How he had her in his power! She looked as if she were going to faint.

"Be brave," I said to her.

She began to cry.

"I thought you were willing to marry him," said Little Yellowman to her, "but if you're not . . ." Whatever else he said, I couldn't hear it, what with her crying and sobbing.

"Are you willing to marry this man?" said he, "say yes or no."

"To marry this man?" said she through her tears and surprise.

"Yes, marry this man, I say, are you willing?"

She didn't speak. She thought we were both mocking her, although we were not. Little Yellowman was in deadly earnest.

"She is embarrassed in front of you," I said, " but she was fully agreeable to marry me this morning. Weren't you now?" I asked, turning to her.

"I w-a-a-s," she said, drying her eyes.

"It's a match, then," said little Yellowman,"but I want everything to be in proper order. Let us have witnesses," said he, "that this man is willing to marry this woman. Let us have witnesses," said he, "that she is satisfied to marry him. Let us have it in black and white. Let us have it signed and sealed by the betrothed couple," and he drew a large paper out of his pocket. He sat down at the table, and wrote slowly and carefully.

He gave a loud whistle. One or two of the troupe came in.

"Call the whole troupe," he ordered.

They were called in. The lady who was dressed like a fairy queen came in, and the man who led her horse; so did the keepers of the animals; the musicians came; in came the two mechanics, black and greasy; the clowns came; and the women and children, all tingling with excitement, which Little Yellowman affected not to notice.

He read out the page. That I was willing to marry the woman — that was all. I put my name to it. The Fat Lady signed it shyly. Two others witnessed it and he put it carefully in his pocket.

Some of the people there were knocking great fun out of the whole business. And you would have thought from my demeanour that I was the happiest man in Ireland, as I held the Fat Lady's hand.

"You all have a lot of work to do now," said Little Yellowman to the troupe, "but, tonight at eleven o'clock, as soon as the night's work is done, let you all come over here, every mother's son and father's daughter of you, and if we don't have sport and fun and games, my name isn't Alf Trott."

The people were beginning to leave.

"We'll have a great night — a great night altogether," he said to them, and, for myself, I knew that he was telling the truth.

It will be a great night, if I can make it so.

Chapter Thirteen

About half an hour before the gates were due to open, who should come in to me but Little Yellowman. He looked as if he were very pleased indeed with himself, with the match he had made for me, and with the whole world. He didn't forget to wash his hands in the air; he didn't forget to wink an eye at me, and when you saw him winking, and when you saw the smile that came to his lips and the way the tip of his long hooked nose and the point of his chin were trying to kiss each other, you could not help but laugh, if it were the last laugh left to you. There was a lamp hanging from a rail above our heads, and the way the light was falling on his yellow face, and on the comicality and craftiness in that face, you might have said that he had been put specially into the world to put people into fits of laughter. Anyway, I burst out laughing myself, even though I had planned to play a trick on him. Then he burst out laughing too. We roared laughing together. You could hear us all over the field. He sat down beside me without any invitation. He began digging me in the ribs with his elbow. I started to do the same to him. We roared with laughter again, but little did the rogue know what was the real reason for my merriment.

At last, his speech returned.

"I am delighted, my son," he said," that you have got her at last."

I didn't speak, pretending to be shy.

"Even if she is a bit fat ," said he, "is she not the better for it?"

I had already decided what to do. I was determined to knock some fun out of the situation for myself, if I could.

"I should never have been attracted to her at all," said I "if she were not a bit on the stout side. Stout women . . ."

"Ah! Stout women! Stout women!" he interrupted enthusiastically, "they are the nicest. They are the kindest, the most affectionate, the gentlest, the quietest, the most sensible, the most understanding. Never will you find them creating any trouble or mischief. They accept life as it is. Their disposition is always happy, sunny, content. They always put the company at ease. If I were to marry, I should only marry a stout woman. No other."

He started thumping me again in the ribs with his elbow, nudging and winking. I was between wanting to laugh and choking the villain to death. But in the end, the urge to laugh got the better of the urge to throttle.

"Only that I was afraid she wouldn't be willing . . ." I began, but had to stop myself, in case he might think I were joking.

"Afraid she wouldn't be willing?" said he, completely surprised. "She is willing, my son, more than willing. There is not a man on earth she would exchange for you. You are the white-headed boy, the man of the moment, the only man in her life. You are her own choice."

"What a storyteller you are!" said I.

"Ah! You rogue," said he, and closed one eye, keeping it closed this time, and giving me another dig in the ribs. "Ah! You rogue," he said, "I had you spotted for a long time. But I never thought you could be such a seducer. It would never have occurred to me. And how well you were able to pick out the right one! (Another dig in the ribs.) Stout women! I shall have to avoid them myself. They are dangerous . . . very dangerous!"

There was a little window high-up in the wooden wall of my booth and I had seen somebody looking in at us. It was the Fat Lady herself; she had obviously come to visit me, and to discuss our engagement before the show was due to open, but, when she saw Little Yellowman she ran off as fast as she could. He had not noticed her there.

"But once the wedding is over," said I after a while, " you will have to give my wife a proper wage."

"Of course. It will only be your entitlement . . . but I'll tell you what I'll do . . ."

He paused, and looked at me sharply between the two eyes. It wasn't a kindly, honest look, but the look that a cat might give a mouse, if she were afraid it might escape from her into its hole. Since then, I have always called that look "Little Yellowman's look."

"Once the wedding is over," he said, "I shall give you five pounds a week between you. Five pounds! I shall put the two of you into the same accommodation. I shall announce your marriage to the world . . . but you will have to give me a contract that you will both stay with me for at least two years."

I knew well what he had in his mind. If he could get me in his grip, if he could make an exhibition of frightfulness and terror out of me before the whole world, he would be winning. I said nothing, for fear I should let him know what was in my mind. He talked and he talked, as if he were addressing a huge crowd of people who had come to see "The Wild Man" — and his wife — "The Fat Lady."

"The Fattest Lady in the World," he intoned, "twenty-seven stone weight. The Fat Lady who married the Wild Man who killed eight men in Germany with his knife! See the traces of blood on it still! And how happy they are together! Ah! Young ladies, isn't love wonderful? How well the Irish poet, Thomas Moore, expressed the fact that there is nothing on earth so powerful as love! Don't you agree, young ladies?

And if you do, ask those young gentlemen what they

think. But wait, how did the poet say it? . . . Ah! May God help me! My memory is not as good as it used to be . . ."

He looked around him. You would think by him that he was seeing something far away in the distance, something wonderful that no one else could see. He seemed to remain in a trance for several minutes, without saying another word.

"Love!" he exclaimed at last, and spread out both arms. "Love! For how much trouble and dissension, how many combats and battles, how much war and slaughter has it not caused since history began? And there is no respite from it. Ah! Love! Eternal as the hills, glorious as the sun . . . has it changed at all since the days of the sons of Uisneach? No, my dear friends, hasn't even the Wild Man here got a Deirdre of his own? He has, and loves her more than . . . Oh! If you wait another few minutes, you will all be kissing each other . . . Ah! Ah! Isn't love wonderful?"

Every time he pronounced the word "love," he would close his eyes, and you would think from his pouted lips that he was sucking honey. If he could manage to make the same speech to the punters, and to deliver it with the same fluency, I was in no doubt but that they would come flocking in to him in their thousands. But a poet cannot compose a beautiful poem every time he feels like it; the gift of poetry was stronger in Little Yellowman on this day than it had ever been before. His heart was uplifted; the uplift of heart that comes to a poet when he declaims his own poetry.

"Five pounds," I said, in a low voice, but just loud enough for him to hear, and I said it in such a way as to make him believe that I was thinking about the money all the time, and that I was fully satisfied with the pay.

"Five pounds," he said, in a more poetic way than he had ever spoken about love. "Five pounds, it's big money; you will make your fortune."

"You won't fail to make some yourself," I said, with a

wink, "the whole world will be coming to see us."

"I might make a little," said he, innocently, "although I'm afraid that I am fated to die without a crumb in my mouth . . . but here, they are in on top of us already."

I was decked out and equipped. The door of the booth was opened. Little Yellowman squared himself up for work. He stood in the doorway.

"Roll up! Roll up! The Wild Man! The Wild Man! Killed eight men with his long sharp knife. See the bloodstains on it still!" And on and on like that to coax the people in.

But he took the opportunity to say to me, before the people came in, that it was no good speaking about an exhibit, if you did not speak poetically; that the Irish were a poetic people, that no political leader had ever done any good for country or people if he had not something of the poet in him, that he had met a poet that evening in a public house, and that he had agreed to buy a poem from him for thirty shillings — a long poem in praise of the betrothal; that he was going to learn it off by heart, so that the audience would think he was composing it while he was reciting it, just as the old Irish poets used to do.

"'Five pounds," said I.

"Five pounds," said he.

"Under your hand and seal," said I.

"Under my hand and seal," said he.

Chapter Fourteen

It is ten o'clock. The booth is full to overflowing. The people are packed in tightly together like herrings in a barrel. Some of them are so far away from me that I can't see them. Little Yellowman is there, busy trying to make room for them all, and for those who are still outside.

When he has got everybody sorted out, he stands up on a box in the centre of the crowd.

"Ladies and Gentlemen," he said, "People of Galway," he said, "I have a small but special word for you tonight. You will all have seen my Fat Lady. She is not my wife. As you know, I have not been married yet . . ." "You are time enough." said a voice from the audience.

"How right you are. I am time enough . . . but Galway is full of lovely ladies." He looked around him. Some of the women began to simper self-consciously.

"But this Fat Lady of mine," he said, looking around him again, and pronouncing each word as if he were a judge pronouncing the death sentence on a criminal, "my Fat Lady, is . . . . in love !"

Everybody laughed.

"But that's not the worst part of the story," said he, dolefully, "hasn't she given the love of her heart — and it's she who has the big heart — to a man who is here with us tonight." He looked intently at a young man who was standing near him. Everyone stared at the young man, who blushed with embarrassment.

"Upon my soul, Peter," said his companion, "right enough, you have been here every night since they came."

Little Yellowman heard this, and pretended to be saddened by it.

"I must inform you, young man," said he, looking at the youth who had blushed, that I am in *loco parentis* here, if you understand the Latin. As you might put it, I am here in her father's place. But I am more than pleased with the young man. I admire her choice."

The young man who had blushed tried to say something, but didn't succeed.

"He is pleased with her, too. There is no point in my trying to deny who he is. It is this man in here — the Wild Man."

You could have heard a pin fall. Everyone there was staring at me open-mouthed. Little Yellowman was standing on top of the box, silent.

He saw one of the troupe at the door.

"Bring her in," said he.

She was ushered in. And from her walk, and the way she swayed, she was for all the world like a great ship at anchor, heaving on the waves.

People who had not seen her before were visibly shocked. Little Yellowman spoke again.

"People of Galway," he said, "and dear friends, I am inviting you all to come to the wedding. The marriage will not take place for a month, but there there will be one fine wedding feast. It will go on for the month, a month's honeymoon before the wedding. The fun will start tomorrow night and if there are not plenty of laughs, my name is not Alf Trott . . . yes, my friend, there will be no extra charge, admission will cost the same — two pence per person."

One of the clowns was there. He struck up a song in English :

"Bring your own tea and sugar;
Bring your own bread and butter;
But you'll come to the wedding —
Won't you come?"

Everyone there exploded with laughter. They started to jeer at Little Yellowman and his "no extra charge." His back was to me. All the attention of the crowd was upon him, not on myself or on the Fat Lady sitting beside me. I straightened out my good leg. I grabbed the stick at my side, and made a crutch of it. I threw off the the black wig and the shining brass chains. I stood up suddenly.

They were all shocked to see me standing up.

"Permission to speak!" said I at the top of my voice, "permission to speak, my friends!"

Some of the women were afraid of me. Even so, I got my permission. If you could have seen Yellowman. He was stuck to the ground, unable to move.

" My dear friends," I said, "you have all heard what has been said about my engagement. Well, it was all a lie. That rogue over there is incapable of telling anything else. When he put me on exhibition, was it not one big lie? And look at all the money he has conned out of you with his lies since ever he came here. And that knife you saw just now has nothing on it but the blood of a fowl. How cleverly he has been tricking you, people of Galway! What dupes you have been! And as for his other exhibits, most of them are just as false as the one you have been looking at until just now. How easy it was to trick you out of your money! But I'll leave him to explain himself, since there is no better man to do it."

I sat down on the ground, joy in my heart. I had known that I should eventually do him harm, but had never imagined how well I should succeed.

All hell broke loose. Some of the people were only

shouting for their money back, but others, and these were in the majority, wanted nothing less than little Yellowman's blood. He was trapped in the midst of them and was greatly to be pitied. They tore every stitch of his clothes. They pushed and thumped and scratched him. And when they got tired of that, they started to tear the booths apart. They were not going to leave the old thief with a pennyworth of property undamaged. Some of them said they would set the place on fire. But they didn't.

The people out on the fairground heard the racket. So did the members of Yellowman's troupe. Both lots were wondering what was going on in my booth. They tried to come in, but the place was so packed that they were wasting their time. The booth was pulled down. Then the real racket started. The lights went out, and people were thumping each other indiscriminately. When a man drew out at another, he could not be sure if he hit one of his friends or one of Yellowman's troupe.

And there were some who couldn't care less. All they wanted to do, it seemed, was to get a crack at another man's skull with a stick. Little Yellowman managed to escape from the battlefield. Some were still looking for him, and when they didn't find him, thought that others were protecting him. Then it would be battle between the two factions. In the end, it was not one big battle between the swindled patrons and Yellowman's troupe, but it was as if a hundred single-handed combats were going on all over the field.

I stayed out of it. I was trying to find Little Yellowman and show them where he was hiding.

The field was eventually cleared. Once people realised that the members of the troupe had retired from the fray for some time, peace reigned once more.

I was walking around the field, when some of the troupe came up to me in a hurry. They said the honest showman was half-dead from loss of blood. He had no further use for me. He would give me my money if I would leave immediately. Would I not do well to catch the twelve o'clock train?

I agreed to do just that. I had only a quarter of an hour to catch the train, but catch it I did. Looking out of the window, as the train was pulling away from the platform, I saw a big fat lady standing by the wall under a lamp. She was crying her eyes out.

*   *   *   *   *

If ever you go to Galway, ask about our circus, and you shall have fun. Little Yellowman left that city, at some time of the night, and hardly left it with his blessing.

Chapter Fifteen

London again! That great and terrible city that forever stretches its tentacles out towards people who are hundreds, thousands, of miles away, and draws them inexorably towards her, in spite of themselves, and remakes them in her own image, to swallow them up, to recreate them.

And I was making for the place as fast as the steam-engine could carry me. Shall I fare out well there? I shall have the three months' pay from little Yellowman. And have I not now experience enough to take on the same kind of job? I was full of courage, but, at the same time, I had the feeling, while I sat in that train that I was not doing myself any good. I had a premonition of bad times, and of a bad end, even though my mind, my intelligence and my understanding were telling me that success would follow my journey, they were telling me that I was right to be going there, to make my way in life, telling me that I should eventually become an achiever.

But another instinct, stronger and more powerful than the mind, more active than the understanding, was prophesying doom at the end of my journey. Had I been able to go back while this turmoil was going on inside me, I should certainly have done so, but the conflict within was still being fought when the train arrived at Euston station.

*   *   *   *   *

My battle with myself is over. Mind and understanding have triumphed over that unnameable and incomprehensible instinct which has been telling me to go back. I am already in the centre of the city. Intelligence is speaking again: have I not now acquired the skills of a trade, something I had not got before I first met little Yellowman? A person would only have to look at me to know what great wealth-potential was in me, provided he knew something about show business. All I would have to do was go to any circus, put on the wig, put the brass chains around my neck and waist, paint my face, and give the roar that Little Yellowman had taught me, and I should have a job on the spot! And hadn't I got the chains, the wig, and the grease-paints in my bag?

There was a great life ahead of me : fame and fortune — enough to provide for me in Ireland in my old age. Go back to my people, as I had been saying to myself on the train? It would be madness. And had I not some money left? And almost twenty pounds still to come from little Yellowman? Couldn't I find a position in any circus, if I wanted it? And what, if anything, could I be doing at home, where I might not even be welcome?

But maybe the yellow devil might not send me my money soon. Maybe I spent too much on the journey. I went into a secluded place, and counted what I had in my purse. I was not too happy with it. But I had enough to keep me for at least two months. But if that yellow-faced tyke does not send me my money before then, what shall I do?

I had not sorted out that question when a strong smell of meat came on the wind, tempting me across the street. I was hungry. I had eaten little since leaving Galway, and badly needed a good meal. I crossed over and went into the eating house, and tackled the food that was put before me with relish and gusto.

I had hardly finished the food, when I noticed two men

sitting at a table near me, talking animatedly. One of them was a big man, a big bony man; the other was small and spare, and although he was not saying much himself, he appeared to be keeping the other talking. Once in a while he would wink at the big man, and when he did that, the other would let loose a torrent of words.

They were too far away for me to hear any word of their conversation, but it seemed to me, somehow, that I had met that bony man before. I seemed to recognise him by his manner of speaking, although I could not tell what he was saying. At last he looked in my direction. He clapped his hands. A smile came over his face. He stood up.

"It's you," he said, coming over to me.

I recognised him the minute he spoke to me. Who was it but the man who had presented me with the little wheelchair on that day long ago in the lodging-house. I shook hands with him. It gave my heart a lift to meet such a generous and decent man again. What a good omen it was to meet a man like him on my first day back in London.

He stood in front of me. He welcomed me. Where had I been? What had I been doing? Had I been successful? He asked me a hundred questions, one after the other, before I had a chance to answer any of them. His words came so fast, and there were so many swear-words among them, that anybody listening might have thought that he was in a rage, and was having a fierce argument with me. But he was not. None of his bad language was to be taken literally, and his swear-words did not possess their normal meanings. His language needed them in the same way as embroidery is needed on some women's clothes, for embellishment only. He used coarse words in his speech as a form of polish, in the same manner as a poet may use a high-flown word to ornament the music of his poem. The poor man was not well-educated; and, since he had not been provided with the means of expressing his generous good-heartedness, who could blame him for inventing his own?

I had not been more than ten minutes in his company when he had my whole story, fully and accurately.

"Come with me," said he, "and I will put you on the right road; I have been a long time waiting to get my hands on that thieving little yellow-faced rogue."

"Do you know him?" I asked.

"I certainly do," said he, "I know him from old, my son. But where did you meet him?"

I told him.

"And he owes you a quarter's pay?"

"He does."

"And did he offer you any money when you were leaving?"

"He said he would send it on to me."

"And you have witnesses, I hope."

"I have."

"He will have to send it to you. Here, grab your hat, and come with me."

He took me to a lawyer's office. He explained my case to the lawyer. The lawyer listened patiently. He knew him well, apparently, for he had brought many people to him previously, who were looking for redress.

The lawyer asked me a few questions. He already had little Yellowman's name in his book. According to him, he was nothing but a crook. But he would frighten him. He would give him the shivers. He would lighten his big purse. He had got money out of him before, and would again, if there was a law in the land.

He had written down all I had told him, and began to read it back to me.

"Have I got the whole story, now?" he asked.

"Except for the engagement," I said.

"What engagement?" he asked, "you told me nothing about an engagement."

"I didn't think there was any need to. It was only a trick I played on him." And I laughed out loud when I thought of the way I had made a fool of little Yellowman. But the lawyer was not satisfied until I had told him the whole story. The big bony man was having fits of laughter as he listened to me, but not even a smile came on the face of the lawyer.

"And you signed your name to it. . . . didn't you?" he pressed.

"I did."

"And did anybody witness it?"

"I'm afraid he has you by the . . . unless you are prepared to marry the young lady."

"She is not a young lady," I interrupted him angrily.

"Be that as it may . . . but I shall do my best for you. Never fear but I shall."

"You are a great joker," said the big man to me, "of course, there was no engagement?"

I started to laugh. The other two thought me very humorous indeed.

"Don't be in any doubt but you will get what is due to you," said the lawyer, and he began to write.

We bade him good-bye, and left his office.

Chapter Sixteen

I am back in my former lodgings where the hospital had originally fixed me up. I am back in my old room, and that little picture of the three young men drinking happily is still on the wall. As I look at those three young men (and you would think by the way the sun is shining on them, that they were her special favourites), I am trying to puzzle out why the people of this house have made me so welcome. I was never kind or generous. I had rarely spoken to them. All I had ever done was bid them the time of day, as I went out in the morning and came home in the evening, and salute them whenever I met them. But of course I had the money then. I had been able to pay my way. I did not owe them a penny. The welcome, of course, is not for me, but for the money they think I have.

I wondered what sort of a welcome they would have given me had they known that my money was all spent. I have not a fluke left. The landlady has already been expecting money from me. She hasn't asked me for it yet, not in so many words. Maybe she has been thinking that, whilst I have money, I do not want to give it to her; that I am not being honest. It was only when I first came to this house that anybody ever thought me to be a gentleman. I had always had plenty of money, until now, that is, and the people here had never known me to do a day's work. No wonder, then, that the landlady thought I was somebody important.

I had no great regard for her, but, even so, I did not want to disabuse her of her good opinion of me. I preferred to put off that evil day.

But to do that, I should need to have money. How could I lay my hands on it? For a month now I have not let a day go by without paying a visit to the lawyer. But every day it was the same story. He could not find trace or tidings of the little yellow-faced rogue or of his circus. But, whilst he had no idea where in the world he might be, he was certain that he had received the first letter. There was no point in my going to see him again, for the time being. The lawyer was getting tired of me. The landlady was getting tired of me. I did not know when I might be evicted from the house. Neither of them would have any respect for me until my pockets were full again. There is a fundamental difference between a rich cripple and a poor one.

There was a knock at the door of my room. It was sure to be the landlady looking for her rent. I pretended to be asleep, in the hope that she would go away. Not a bit of it. She knocked again.

While I was in bed, the wooden leg was on a chair beside me. I hated anyone to see it there. I pushed it in under the bed.

"Come in." I shouted to whoever was at the door.

The landlady put her head in.

"There is a man at the door who says he has business with you; he says he won't go until he sees you."

"What kind of man is he?" I asked, afraid it might be Little Yellowman himself. If it were . . .

"A big bony foul-mouthed man," said she.

"Let him in," said I.

It was, of course, himself, the big man who had given me the wheelchair long ago. He sat down at the foot of the bed.

"I have two letters for you," he said. "The lawyer gave them to me. I knew that yellow-faced rogue would take fright; I knew he would be forced to part with the money. I made no mistake in bringing you to the lawyer. He is able to . . . "

"Give me the letters." I interrupted him.

He took them out of his pocket. He laid them on the bed.

I had my money at last! I should be able to pay my way. I should not have to go begging. I should not have to turn to crime. I spent a good while just looking at the letters, pondering on one thing after another. A quarter's pay! Almost forty pounds! I was rich, I should never see another poor day.

"Open them," said the big man.

I took one of them and opened it. No money fell out.

"This is not from little Yellowman," I said.

"Who else, then?"

I looked at the letter again. It was signed by the big Fat Lady. My soul almost left my body.

"Now the other one," said the big man, and handed me the second letter. I opened it. No money in it either. I wasn't able to read it. All I saw was a cloud of small black characters swimming before my eyes.

The big man started to read the first letter. He began to laugh, and every peal of his laughter could be heard at the other side of the street.

"Upon my soul, but I never thought you were that kind of a fellow. Devil a bit of it. Isn't she really stuck on you? So loving and affectionate! And me thinking all the time that you took no interest in women! But listen to this! Just listen to it!" and he started to read aloud.

"Dear little brother, dear little son of my heart. Be careful. He is after you. The little man is after you. He will never be satisfied. He will never have a night's sleep, until he has taken your life. He has sworn and pledged himself that one or other of you, you or he, will be dead in a very short time. He went down on both knees one night in the middle of the road, in front of the whole troupe, the Bible in his hand, his head bare in the moonlight, oh, if you had seen him, he would have struck terror into your heart. Oh, if anything dreadful should happen to you, after all the love we have given one another . . ."

As bad as was my predicament, I couldn't help laughing. The big man gave another roar.

"Read it out," I said.

He began again . . .

". . . But you had no right to ruin a fine circus which had been on the road for so many years. And that is what you did. Our bad reputation went before us everywhere — people were saying that everything in it was fake. There were letters to the papers — and would you believe it? One letter said that I was a fraud — that I was not half the weight that was claimed for me. I thought at first that it was you who were writing the letters, but when I read that one, I knew I was mistaken, for you would never tell a lie, and there is no man alive better placed to know my correct weight than yourself. But without you, I am losing weight daily. There won't be a pick left on me if you don't come back to me, or send over for me . . ."

The big man looked at me. There was humour in his eyes, but I could see nothing funny about the situation. I felt he was laughing at me, and I didn't like it. I snatched the letter from him.

"She is really in love with you," he said, "you would do yourself nothing but good by marrying her."

"The devil take my soul, if you don't stop . . ."

"A loving affectionate girl, in failing health without you, in danger of death from grief and a broken heart!" "There won't be a pick left on me if you don't send for me," said he.

I threatened him with my crutch. He only laughed. He didn't think I was in earnest, but drew away from me, all the same.

"A beautiful young lady — of course she has to be beautiful — a lovely graceful young lady in danger of death for love of him, and he will not send for her! He won't even send her news of his good health, and that he is on his guard. How shameful, how dreadfully shameful! And you engaged to her as well! How dense I was when you told us in the lawyer's office that you were engaged. Come, man, come! You'd best marry her!"

After finishing his speech, the big man slumped back in his chair, and went into fits of laughter. I had the other letter in my hand, and I was reading it. It was from little Yellowman's lawyers, threatening to sue me for Breach of Promise on behalf of the Fat Lady, and for the slanderous letters that I had sent to the newspapers insulting Little Yellowman and disparaging his circus. I should not get my pay until both of these matters had been settled. The sooner they were settled, the better it would be for me. Little Yellowman would accept the amount of pay due to me in settlement of his claim, but I should have to settle with the Fat Lady in another way.

The big man brought the two letters to the lawyer, to deal with both matters on my behalf. Yellowman would have to settle his account with me, whatever about the affair of the Fat Lady.

"Take courage; you shall get your money eventually," said the big man as he left, but the poor man didn't know that I was in no position to wait, that I hadn't a red penny in the world, and that I was already hungry. My courage began to fail as he left. I began to despair. Why had I the misfortune to come over here again? If only I had stayed at home? Had there been a bridge between the two islands, I should walk across it, even though I have only one leg.

A cripple passed by outside. I could recognise the sound of his sticks on the paving stones. I suppose he was begging, or selling small items of merchandise. I almost went over to the window to see him, to see what my own situation would shortly be. But I didn't leave the bed. I didn't once put my wooden leg under me that day, or until the next morning, thinking, thinking, and they were not happy thoughts, but bitter depressing ones, morbid gloomy reflections on the injustice of poverty, and on the inequalities in society, painful thoughts which cut into a person's heart and change him into a creature full of resentment and malice.

I was hungry that night, with a hunger that was not only of the body, but of heart and mind and soul.

Chapter Seventeen

I didn't leave the house for two day, and had hardly anything to eat. On the third day I got up and went out. I had decided I should not return until I had enough money to pay the landlady, be it sooner or later.

I thought at first that I should make my way to the lawyer's office to see if he might have another letter for me, but when I looked at the clock I saw that it was not yet nine, and his office would not be open so early. There was a large park nearby, and I went in to while away a couple of hours. It was the Indian summer of St. Michael's day, and the sun was as warm and bright as if it were the beginning of August. There were not many people about, as it was so early in the morning, except in one corner of the park. That corner was so crowded that you would not have room to move in it. It was black with people, all lying on the ground. They were all homeless, vagrant people. Most of them were lying face down on the ground. Some of them lying on their backs, their faces to the sky. Some asleep. Others awake. A man here cursing and swearing loudly enough to split the rocks of the Burren. Another over there stretching his limbs and scratching himself: and you would think by him that he was engaged in important and serious business.

Whilst their ragged clothing would not protect them from the icy winds of winter, neither did they keep out the grateful warmth of the sun's rays. "If you have no fire, warm yourself by the sun," seems to be the motto of all of them.

I could only liken this corner of the park to some huge hateful giant who was suffering from some hideous loathsome disease, a dreadful disease that was rotting his flesh, and gnawing it to the bone, visible in great black spots erupting from his skin. It seemed to me that the pain he was suffering from the disease had turned his skin grey, and that the black spots were quivering from time to time from some turbulence in his bloodstream.

I, too, started sunning myself on the breast of that diseased, detestable giant.

* * * * *

I am paying no attention to the black spots on his skin. I am lying on my back, surrounded by large trees. The wind is murmuring in the treetops. The leaves are singing a blithe and tuneful song, but a different song to the one they were singing at the start of summer. Their merriment is of a different kind in this, the season of dying. Whenever a little breeze rustles the shrivelled leaves, they make a noise like a death rattle, but the ones that are still green keep on dancing joyfully, happy that they are still able to resist the death which is in store for them. A withered leaf falls on my forehead. I let it stay where it fell. Another falls on my mouth. They are now falling about me thick and fast. And the homeless men who dot the grass around me seem like huge withered leaves, fallen from some great tree . . .

A blade of grass is growing beside my ear. It tickles my ear when the wind catches it, and I pretend that it is a live thing, trying to get a look at me. This blade of grass makes me angry. I stretch out my hand to pull it up. There is a long-legged yellow insect clinging, half-dead, to the tip of it. When I shake the stem, the insect falls to the ground and puts up its legs to defend itself. I become aware of a great number of similar creatures, all with that half-dead appearance. They are preparing themselves for their winter's sleep. If only I could hibernate myself! I pull the blade of grass and put it into my mouth. I chew it like a cow, without admitting to myself that I am very hungry indeed.

Hunger! But why am I so hungry? Didn't I eat a meal yesterday? And maybe the money is waiting for me in the lawyer's office. Little Yellowman can hardly be entitled to hold onto it. That letter he wrote can only have been a ploy. Wasn't it my money? But I shall leave it lie in the lawyer's office for a month, for three months, for a year, if I feel like it. If I were to go asking for it now, the rogue of a lawyer might only think that I was desperate for it.

Unconsciously, I tightened my belt around my waist. I kept on chewing the blade of grass until it coloured my mouth green.

A clock strikes. A church clock somewhere. I listen to each stroke. One — two — three — four . . . But surely it can't be four yet. It was only after nine when I came in here. The lawyer will be gone home. I won't get my money today. I must hurry.

I stand up suddenly and hurry off as fast as my wooden leg will allow me. My head is dizzy. I am like a drunken man, swaying from side to side on the crutch. I am drunk, all right — drunk with hunger. The strange futile thoughts that have been coming into my head, and going away like the wind, have been drunken thoughts, the thoughts of a madman. Could I reach the park gate by hitting my crutch against the ground only a certain number of times? If I could, Little Yellowman's money would certainly be waiting for me in the lawyer's office. If I could not, I should be without it. I made a determined effort to reach the gate without striking the ground with the crutch more than forty -seven times. What an effort! What an exhausting march! Sweat was pouring off me and the sun beat down on me without mercy. I was an object of pity, of contempt, as I turned and twisted my body to get to the gate.

The wind blew my hat off. A child on his way home from school put it back on my head. A lot of people were staring at me, with surprise or concern.

When I was nearly ten yards from the gate, I was certain that I had struck the ground with the crutch forty-three times. Only four strokes left. But I couldn't do it. I was almost crying, but I thought of a stratagem. I struggled ahead on one hand and one knee. I threw the crutch away. I had reached the gate having only touched the ground with it forty-three times. I should get the money. And wouldn't I know how to spend it!

What should I get to eat? A chicken? It would not be at all bad! Yes, I should certainly get a chicken. A chicken and a piece of bacon, and some cabbage, if it could be had at all. I took no interest in the food that I saw in the shop windows as I made my way along. It would be tasteless. No, it must be a chicken, nothing less! I kept on saying this to myself seventeen times, like a child repeating a lesson. But before I had got my thinking under control I was at the lawyer's office.

There was nobody in the office only the clerk. He looked at me.

"Were you not told that the money would be sent on to you if it came?" said he.

"I was not ."

"It will be . . . But wait. Where are you living?"

I had already decided not to go back to the lodgings. I gave him the first address that came into my head, and left.

I had only got outside the door when I realised what I had done. Now, if the money were sent to me, somebody else would get it. I called myself a fool, an idiot and many other names. The intoxication of hunger and the madness that had taken possession of me in the park had by now left me. The hunger itself had disappeared. I went back into the park. I began to be afraid. I started crying, and soon fell asleep.

It was night when I awoke. But I could tell, from the noises of the city that came towards me in the park, that it was still early. After the hot day, the night had come down cold, as is usual in October. My clothes were not too bad, but, even so, I could feel the cold penetrating my bones.

I walked quickly across the park, like somebody who had important business to do. I had only one thought in my head, and that was how best to go about getting something to satisfy my hunger. "Hunger is the best sauce," I said to myself, and laughed out loud. The passers-by stared at me in amazement.

I see a piece of bread lying on the edge of the pavement. Maybe a child dropped it on its way to school. I grab it. I clean it on the skirts of my coat. I eat half of it gratefully and with a blessing and I put the other half away in my pocket, first wrapping it in a piece of paper.

There is a brightly-lit public house in front of me. A crowd of men are standing with their backs to the wall. They remind me of those gadflies that suck the blood of horses and cattle. I stood among them nonchalantly, just as though I had been standing there since the beginning of time. There was a tall thin man, with pock-marked cheeks, standing beside me.

I felt like talking. Remember I had not spoken a word to anybody for two days, except for the few words I had had with the clerk.

"Was Alf Trott here today?" I asked (you will remember that that was the name of Little Yellowman).

The man was surprised when I spoke to him.

"Trott — Trott — Alf Trott — Alf Trott," and he repeated the name twenty times as if it were reminding him of something.

Some of the others had also heard my question.

One of them began to say the word "Trott" over and over again, as if he were gaining great satisfaction out of it.

Another started up "Trott" — "Trott" — "Trott," and yet
another with "Trott" — "Trott" — "Alf Trott."

There wasn't one of them who wasn't bemused by the
name. Some were saying he had been there that morning.
Others that he had not been there since the day before
yesterday. I was afraid they might be coming to blows over
it.

"Isn't he the big fat man who comes in every evening to
play cards?" said one.

"He's not," said another, "he's the little skinny fellow
who is always with him."

"The fat man's name isn't Trott," said the man I spoke to
first, "it's Cox."

"And the small man's name is Box," said I, trying to be
funny, "Their names are Box and Cox."

They were surprised by this. It had never occurred to
them that those two might be named Box and Cox. They
started to discuss the pair. There was one man there who
knew where Cox worked. But another man was certain that
the same fellow had never done a day's work in his life.

They were making me deaf. I left them there, to their
discussion of Cox and Box and Trott.

*   *   *   *   *

But it is very cold, and the vicious pain is back in my
stomach. I chew the other bit of bread. The crust is as hard
as a stone, but I like it the better for that, I have so little of it.
I get great satisfaction out of getting my teeth into it. I tuck
my coat around me and hurry on until I begin to sweat, until
I am ready to collapse with fatigue, until my one leg is
starting to give way, my armpit bruised and sore from the
crutch, so that I shall have to rest somewhere. I sit down on
the big seat by the river (on the spot where I first gave little
Yellowman's howl, that night long ago when I went astray

in the fog) but I am too weary and exhausted to notice this ; I am too tired to be aware of the great black river sliding past me like a huge horrendous serpent. I don't even see that great serpent with its myriad lights, its myriad eyes, the thousand precious stones glistening in its skin. I do not marvel at it one bit. I marvel only at myself.

*   *   *   *   *

It was dawn when I awoke. I don't know what woke me, but I felt that somebody had stuck a dagger in my stomach. Indeed, I couldn't be sure I had not been stabbed until I opened my coat and shirt. There was no sign of any blood. It was a good while before I admitted to myself that I was suffering from the pangs of hunger, and realised that I had been awakened by a policeman passing by.

*   *   *   *   *

I stood up and went for a walk, hoping to think of some plan of action. In other large cities, when a person is in dire straits, it will not occur to him that the objects around him, the houses, the walls, the streets themselves, have any evil designs on him, but in London such a person would be inclined to think that the great gloomy houses would knock him down — would fall on him — crush him, if they could be bothered with a creature so insignificant.

I was now in a district of large hotels. People were searching through the dustbins which were left outside each hotel. Mostly old people, men and women, and when one of them found a piece of bread, or a bit of meat, you could see them clutching it in their skinny, bony fingers, and scraping the dirt off the filthy morsels with their nails .   .   . As they bent over the galvanised bins, in the dim light of the dawn, and the great hotel buildings glowering down on them with disdain, they were like a flock of great ravenous desert birds, savage and hideous, stripping human bones with their dreadful talons. Watching them, a shiver went through me, as if somebody were scraping glass.

The Big Red-haired Woman! At the thought of her I began to see a way out. I could visit her anytime! I rushed off. As happy as if I had found the key of Heaven in my pocket. My heart was full. The Big Red-haired Woman would surely have a welcome for me. Maybe that great-hearted woman with the face like a Roman emperor would be the means of my salvation.

And she would have, only that her room was cold and empty when I got there. It looked as if nobody had lived in it for years. I began to feel lonely. My heart filled with sadness that that woman who had once comforted me like a mother was not there to welcome me. And I had so looked forward to her hearty welcome! I sat down on the floor, on the very spot where we had sat together by the firelight on that foggy night so long ago. Like the Children of Lir, I composed a poem, although its words were my tears. I wept and wept and wept until the tears were blinding me. I don't know of anything, apart from laughter, that can do so much to lift a human heart as weeping, especially when tears come gently and easily, as they came to me on this blessed morning. My own tears came so gently and easily that they did me a world of good.

The reek and the snorting of the horses were coming up through the chinks in the timbers. There was a man down there too, sweeping the flagstones. Sweeping, sweeping, sweeping, and it seemed to me that nobody had ever worked so hard with a sweeping brush since Eve first picked a bunch of heather to clean her dwelling. This sweeping was upsetting me so much that I knew my hunger was still tormenting me, even though there had been a respite from the pain. Between any two bouts of hunger pains I had been making too much of small annoyances like this, and allowing them to upset me. Another bout would not be long coming. What form would it take? I had ceased to notice whether the man below in the stable was sweeping or not. It was the next bout, and only that, which was worrying me. I had never before gone without food for so long. Nausea? No, you couldn't have nausea with nothing in your stomach . . . but maybe the man below might know the whereabouts of that Big Red-haired Woman with the face of a Roman emperor — if he did, I should be in luck.

Chapter Eighteen

When I saw him for the first time, I was seized with a mixture of dislike and pity and disgust at the ugliness of his form and features. He was an old man — a tiny dwarfish old man who was so bent and twisted that you would think he would break in half if you attempted to straighten him. You would imagine that his face had been carved out of granite rock, but that the sculptor had grown sick and tired of its ugliness, and had given it up as a bad job, leaving it to bleach under the wind and sun of eternity.

If there was a thought in him, other than one based on cunning and treachery, it did not manifest itself in that wrinkled stony face. His brush, which he held in his hand with the grip of a drowning man, was much taller than him. He stood still as a statue. Like a spectre created by some mischievous fiend, as a mocking caricature of all humankind. He had been given some of the shape and make of a person. Surely the brush had been placed in his hand to prove that he was not really human, but the sort of beast that man might have been but for the goodwill of our Creator.

He was one of those dreadful examples, that may be seen now and again, of what we humans might have been like if some different developments had occurred in the process of our evolution. That ironic man of loves and hatred, Jonathan Swift, may indeed have seen a creature like him before writing his baleful satire of Gulliver among the Yahoos.

The horses were so graceful, so well-formed, with their

smooth shining coats, so spirited, so lively, so well-nourished and groomed . . . and he! How hideous he was, with his shoulders out of symmetry, his misshapen twisted body bent in two, and the tool of his trade, his big long-handled brush, which made him look all the smaller, the more insignificant, the more hideous — and those two sunken eyes — probably with little sight in them! Ugh! . . .

I was filled with disgust. Could I find some way of touching his heart? If I were to give a roar — Yellowman's roar — might it frighten him? If I were to strike him in the face, would he defend himself?

(The next bout of hunger had arrived. I could tell by the feeling of intoxication that was coming over me as I contemplated the man with the brush. I tried to banish the strange thoughts that were welling up in me like a spring flood. I succeeded in keeping them under control for a while).

The man with the brush had remained completely motionless all this time.

"Hey!" I shouted.

He put his hand to his ear. He was deaf. I moved towards him. He was filthy dirty with horse-dung, reeking with his own stench and the smell of the horses' sweat.

"Can you hear me?" said I.

He made no move. He was definitely deaf.

"Hey!" I shouted again, this time into his ear. It was no use, although I had shouted at the top of my voice. And, I tell you, with the breath I drew, I had greatly hurt my empty stomach.

The strange thoughts started to come back to me again. I couldn't keep them away. But I kept one thought firmly in the back of my head, how to find out where the Big Red-haired Woman lived.

I roared again into the man's ear. The horses started, but he only shook his head to tell me that he could not hear.

I lost patience.

"May you be seven times worse a year from this night," I said angrily, "why didn't you tell me that before? Do you think that I have the time to stay here with you all day?"

I left him there. Himself and his big brush! There was a bag of meal just inside the door. I put my hand into it and took out a handful.

There was a young man outside the door, leading two horses. He had just arrived.

"Have you any idea where the Red-haired Woman is, who used to live upstairs?"

"Big Maggie?"

"She's the one I want."

"So far as I know, she's locked up."

"Locked up? "

"Yes, locked up — locked up in prison. Do you understand?"

"Oh! I do."

"That's where she is, all right, if I'm not greatly mistaken. And not a bad place at all to spend the winter . . . If I don't succeed . . . maybe I'll be spending the winter there too . . . and, if you'll take my advice, you'll go there yourself."

I was annoyed with him for thinking I was in so extreme a plight. I was trying to think what I should say to him, so that he should know that I was in no such predicament.

Then he stretched out his hand to me, with a copper penny in his palm.

"Get yourself some bread," said he, "This is all I have."

I took the penny, and didn't even wait to say "thank you." I was terrified in case he might follow me and try to take it back.

When he didn't, another feeling came over me. A feeling of dreadful shame for having accepted his penny. I had accepted money from a horse boy. And had he not insulted me by thinking I was hungry and should be better off in

prison? I had been shamed. Shamed for ever. I had lost my
self-respect for all time. It would have been different if I had
asked for the money. That would have made sense. But to
accept it in the way it had been offered was demeaning. I
made up my mind to go back and throw the dirty money at
him, but then I saw some lovely little loaves in the window
of a shop. They would only be a penny each. And how nice
they looked! You never saw loaves with such beautiful
crusts top and bottom. I praised the man who had kneaded
them. I praised the farmer and his wheat. I praised the fire,
and the men who had taken fuel for it out of the womb of
the Earth. I praised the man who was selling the loaves, and
paid tribute to the honest man in the way he liked best, by
giving him my penny for one of them.

I chew the delicious fresh bread, crusted brown from the
fire.

But how had the horse-boy been able to tell that I was
hungry? (I was still thinking about it, even while eating the
loaf.) I was certainly thin. But doesn't a body lose weight
after a bad bout of illness? Doesn't he often have a weak,
wavering, shuffling walk? A strange look in his eyes? I
looked in a mirror in a shop window. I was astonished,
frightened. I could barely recognise my own appearance. I
laughed out loud (for what reason I don't know now) and I
took to the dirty mean back-streets.

Everything I had been thinking about the man with the
brush this morning could now apply equally to myself.

It angered me when people looked at me. I took it as an
insult. But perhaps they were right, if it were true that I had
been created by some mischievous fiend as a caricature of
the human race, as I had imagined he created the man in the
stable this morning. I stuck out my tongue at everybody
who looked at me, and kept going, making a great noise
with my crutch on the flagstones.

I went into a park. I flung myself on the ground under an

oak tree. My head became dizzy. I lay on my back. I saw hundreds of colours mixing with each other, and making thousands of beautiful multi-coloured pictures, one picture following another with such speed that my brain was mesmerised and tired out by them. When I tried to banish them, music invaded my ears, the sounds of the music changing as rapidly as had the pictures.

Night fell.

Chapter Nineteen

I was startled suddenly before much of the night had passed. Never before had I heard such noise — shouting, screaming and roaring. Crowds and gangs of people were coming across the park. In the direction they were going, the lower part of the sky was red and a great torch of light was rising up into the firmament, like a long narrow tongue trying to suck blood.

I was barely awake when my stomach began to torment me. I put my hand into my pocket, and from the collection of rubbish in it — pebbles, buttons, crumbs, nails and the rest — I fished out a bone button and popped it into my mouth. I began to swallow the saliva that gathered around it. I had discovered that it relieved the severe pain.

The people were going past me in droves. I have often noticed that crowds have a certain way with them. A crowd is like an individual person. When the crowd is angry, it seems that each member of it is angry. It also appears that when the crowd is in joyous mood, so also is each person in it. A person would be inclined to go along with the crowd, such is its power over him. Each little drop of water that makes up a river will always flow in the same direction.

This crowd passing by had the same power over me. I followed it.

At first I had thought of nothing else but just to join in. Then I began to think that I might find food or drink, or some way of getting money. With such a huge number of people, all moving so quickly, it would not be natural if some of them did not lose a purse, a shilling, or even a penny. I kept my two eyes on the ground, which was clearly illuminated by the light from the conflagration, but if anybody had lost anything, I didn't find it. I didn't have that much luck.

It was a great factory building that was on fire. The street in front of it was wide, but was packed with people. There were tall and short there. Rich and poor. Workers and unemployed. Fine important-looking gentlemen in white shirts and tall black hats, on their way home from the theatres. And there were people there, like myself, who were accustomed to taking the night air every night of the year.

The fire brigades were there in their hundreds, squirting great streams of water on to the flames, which, nevertheless were breaking out all over the place, in spite of all their efforts, and leaping ever higher and higher in the sky. As the flames, which were growing stronger and stronger all the time, came in contact with any of the chemical products in the factory, they took on marvellous colours — blood-red, purple, lilac — colours of white, yellow, blue and green, colours which were reflected on the faces of the people around as they watched the blazing inferno.

It was a wonderful sight. There was a small square in front of the factory at the other side of the street. This small square was surrounded by a stone wall, and a number of women who had been working in the factory were standing on top of it. There was considerable discussion going on among these women on the wall.

Some of them were full of good humour, and joy and laughter to see the factory going up in flames. The place had a bad reputation and they had been greatly exploited while working there. But there were others who were crestfallen and sad on account of losing their employment. But the owner of the factory was not half so upset as were his employees. And why should he be? The fire would not leave him any worse off. What was there to upset him when he knew that he would be recompensed for his loss by the Insurance Company? And you never saw such happy people as the ones who were laughing with delight. They were very annoyed with the women who were worried at the prospect of losing their livelihood.

The happy ones reminded the others of the number of their comrades who had died from the effects of the chemical products which they had been manufacturing. They reminded them too, of how much they had suffered there. They scolded them and said that they had no spirit. It looked as if they were ready to hit them. But some of these people were only thinking of all the hardship that they would have to endure again once the factory had been rebuilt.

Among the happy ones, I particularly noticed a big woman. She was very excited, and was encouraging her faction to sing triumphant songs to demonstrate what they thought of the factory, and of the man who owned it. A cheerful song was struck up, and they sang it loudly and triumphantly. And there was hatred in it too. All the hardship, all the exploitation that they had suffered in that factory infused their song with malice. But the note of celebration was louder and sweeter. After all, wasn't the hardship and exploitation over now, at least for some time?

A sudden flash lit up the faces of both the sad and the joyful women. I could hardly believe my eyes, but it was! It was Big Maggie, my old friend, the Big Red-haired Woman, who had been standing on the wall exhorting the women . . . It was she.

I moved up beside her so that I could speak to her.

A flame, the colour of blood, leaped up into the sky. The Big Red-haired Woman gave a great shout. The other women took up the shout — a great roar of joy — and they began to clap their hands. One by one, the women who had been troubled until now began to join in with the others, and the Big Red-haired Woman welcomed each new supporter with another shout.

I tried to speak to her. But she was too excited to hear me.

The flames began to snake around the tall chimney outside the factory, like hundreds of raging serpents.

"Fall! Fall!" roared the Big Red-haired Woman. The others joined her in one great shout.

As the flames made contact with the chemical products in the building, they kept changing colour. They were every colour of the rainbow. White here, yellow there. Blood-red in another corner. It was like magic, how the different colours kept interchanging, and at one stage combined into one great blaze of crimson glory.

"The blood of the poisoned women," I shouted.

The Big Red-haired Woman heard what I said, but didn't know who said it.

"The blood of the poisoned women!" she repeated, shouting at the top of her voice.

The crimson blaze was still leaping up from the factory.

"The blood of the poisoned women!" roared the women with one voice, so that all could hear them. The manager of the factory heard them too, and he shivered in his shoes.

At last, the sky began to brighten in the East. The black ruined walls of the factory could be seen against the sky, like a huge beast in the middle of the sacrificial altar of some savage tribe, with its four hooves sticking up in the air, begging for mercy.

I was becoming just as excited as the women.

"The beast who tortured women is dead!" I shouted.

The saying was taken up. The crowd started shouting it in unison. In the end it became one great roar coming from a thousand throats.

"The beast who tortured women is dead!"

The manager of the burned-out factory came, trying to get the police to clear the street. He was terrified of the dangerous mood of the mob. His factory had a bad reputation. And nothing of it now remained but the blackened walls, of which some had collapsed.

The fires were going out. But now and then a white flame would flare up, as if the fire were reluctant to part with the ill-starred old factory. Every time there was a flare-up the women would shout for joy. The factory manager and the Head Constable were in conversation.

"Throw him to the flames!" cried a woman.

"Throw him to the flames!" shouted another.

By this time the women were in a frenzy of rage. The street had got to be cleared. I saw the Big Red-haired Woman high up on a wall clapping her hands rhythmically; when I looked again she was gone. In the rumpus, I had nearly lost her, but she must have recognised me, for I suddenly felt her two strong arms around my waist, and I was lifted up as if I were an infant, and was being kissed again and again.

It was my Big Red-haired Woman.

The other women workers recognised me. They saw that I was the one who had started the shouting, and wanted to bring me with them to congratulate me. But the Big Woman ordered them to leave me be, as I was an old friend of hers, and, indeed, a relative.

She would not allow me to walk one step. She carried me all the way and, Lord, wasn't she the strong fit woman? — stronger than many a famous athlete.

The others followed us and stayed with us until we reached the Big Woman's house. Even then they wouldn't leave us, but remained outside until daylight, singing songs in my honour.

Chapter Twenty

The Big Woman began: "Oh! Aren't you in a sorry state? You look starved and hungry. How thin you have got, and how you have lost weight! Where have you been, or what has happened to you to leave you in such a desperate condition? You are like a man who has been crushed between two millstones. May the Son of God preserve us! Speak to me, and tell me where you have been all this time. I thought I should never lay eyes on you again — never . . ."

Once that Big Woman started talking, it was hard for anyone else to get a word in edgeways. She would rush her words, almost like a horse galloping. And when she was excited, as she was now, it was impossible to keep up with her. You would have to keep listening attentively if you meant to hear all her words, so thick and fast were they coming from her lips. But she hadn't finished yet.

She held my head, and looked hard at me.

"Oh! Aren't you the image of my dear little brother, little Éamonn, Lord rest his soul? You could be his double. I could have sworn that you were he, but for your accident. Truly, Éamonn was the grand young fellow when he was alive . . ." Tears welled up in her eyes.

" . . . And how often I have been trying to puzzle out why I had so much affection for you — until one night I dreamed that I saw Éamonn's face looking down at me. He was there as surely as you are here now. I thought his face was just above that picture over there, looking at me pitifully. I got the feeling that he was trying to speak to me,

but couldn't, and it was your eyes that were gazing at me.
And his mouth! Oh Lord! He was the only brother I ever
had. If he had lived, I should not be leading a life like this.
However, we must accept the will of God. But I am talking
too much, and maybe . . . Oh, what a fool I am! Sure there
is nothing the matter with you only hunger. Am I right, or
have you eaten hardly anything for a month . . . ?" and
she started to prepare food for me.

I told her my story, but I left out the affair of little
Yellowman, in case I should break out laughing over my
meal.

She laid a large dish in front of me.

"Don't eat too much at first," said she, perhaps a drop of
milk to start with . . . "

"The best thing," said I, a little afraid, in spite of a fierce
desire to gulp down the food.

She fetched the milk, and began to spoon it to me, as you
would feed a small child. After each spoonful, she would lay
her hand on my forehead and start to caress my hair,
murmuring, as if she were talking to herself, things like "my
darling," " my poor little pet," "little brother of my heart."

While I was drinking my milk, she had been warming a
blanket in front of the fire. She told me to wrap it around me
and to lie on the bed while she was washing my shirt.

I did what she told me. She sat on a chair beside the bed.
She held my hand in hers, all the time looking at my
emaciated face, at my long skinny fingers, and at the
swollen blue veins in my hands, my forehead and my neck.
She could tell by them how much hardship I had suffered.
Yes, she understood, and from the way she was moving her
fingers through mine, I felt what great compassion she had
for me, although I did not appreciate it fully until I saw the
look in her eyes. Her look was becoming more loving, more
concerned, more gentle all the time, until you might think
she could not keep it up while just sitting on the chair

beside the bed without a stir.

She couldn't, either. She jumped up suddenly and kissed me.

The hot milk had started to make the blood flow in my veins. I felt what seemed like a kind of sleepiness coming over me. But it wasn't. It was simply that this peacefulness and this feeling of comfort was relaxing me. I closed my eyes, and started to think about this woman, who still had my hand in her grip.

I did not succeed on that occasion in making out what kind of woman she was, but since then I have been comparing her to a dammed-up flood; all her natural energy and ability had been bent and twisted by fate, but never completely destroyed. One of those wonderful women who achieve great fame in the world. A woman who could be devil or saint depending on how Fate might deal with her.

I had remained so quiet that she thought I had fallen asleep. She put her cheek to mine and began to kiss me tenderly and timidly, as if she were trying to do it without my knowing.

"Little brother! little brother!" were the last words I heard before I slept.

I stayed with her for two days. She found me lodgings in the house of an Irishman near her own, and she promised to visit me often.

Chapter Twenty-One

Six months ago, that part of London in which I was now living was, in itself, a little Irish world. The English used to call it Little Ireland. All the people were from the province of Munster, except for the odd one. Some of them had inherited the traditions of bards and poets. All the neighbours knew each other, and not alone that, but they knew the families they had come from. They had all come from the same district in Ireland. They used to have social gatherings in the evenings, where you would find fiddlers and pipers and flute-players.

There would be a man there who could relate the contents of Keating's History of Ireland, as well as a man who knew nothing about it. And if somebody were to disagree with anything the savant said, he would just go to the big trunk he had brought with him from Ireland and take out a parcel wrapped in linen. He would open the parcel and take out a large book in manuscript. And how careful he was of that book! He would then show you in black and white where you had been wrong. And when he closed the book to put it away he would look at you as if to say. 'Now what have you to say for yourself?' But he never said a word. And the daytime trade of this man who spent his evenings reading history and learning poetry was the trade of the pick and shovel.

This small population of exiles in a foreign city kept up the manners and customs of the people of the ancient Irish nation. The Irish heritage of language, music and literature which rich people at home had abandoned in their efforts to imitate the English, who would as soon have seen them at the bottom of the sea, was kept alive by these people. They understood, in their own way that a race should guard the culture which had come down to them from their ancestors and they guarded it like a precious jewel.

The adults kept up their habits, customs and language. But their sons and daughters only preserved their native characteristics, and gradually abandoned the language and a lot of it's musical and literary culture. Their grandchildren lost both the language and culture, and seemed to have retained only the worst of their racial characteristics. And many, naturally, intermarried with the English. People who breed animals will tell you that when one breed is crossed with another, the offspring will inherit the worst characteristics of each. Others, however, take the opposite view.

There is probably much to be said on each side of this argument, but the first group could easily prove their case were they to make the population of this small area of London their sole object of study. When I arrived among them, there were only about forty people among them still alive of those who had come from Ireland after the Great Famine. Some of them had retained a knowledge of the Irish language, its stories and sagas, and there were good musicians among them. But they belonged to the past, and their children and grandchildren were little credit to them.

One of these old men who had come over from Ireland after the Famine was my new landlord, who was known as "Hammer". He was given this nick-name because of his great interest in debate, and of his habit of shouting "Another nail in the plank!" every time be believed he had won an argument. He wore an overcoat, which had belonged to his grandfather, at all seasons of the year. Even in the middle of a heat-wave, he never took off that coat. He usually carried an oak walking-stick — a heavy stick he had cut when he once went back on a week's visit to his native village.

One thing is certain. This man had never done a stroke of work since the day he set up this lodging-house. There were old people in the neighbourhood, who had known his people at home, who said that Hammer was a lazy untrustworthy fellow, just like his forbears. But nobody took any notice of them. In summer, he used sit in his chair outdoors in a spot sheltered from the heat of the sun, and indoors in winter in a spot near the heat of the fire. Outdoors or indoors, he never took off the overcoat, nor left his stick out of his hand. Irishmen in the district who were too old to work made a habit of coming by for a bit of debate, which would always end with, "another nail in the plank" from Hammer.

Whether or not Hammer was lazy, his wife Brigid certainly was not. It was she who did the housekeeping. If the rooms were clean, and the beds made, it was she who cleaned and made them. If she didn't prepare meals for the two of them, they would have gone without food. If she did not wash the clothes, they would never have been washed. And, even when all these jobs were done, she would still not have finished her day's work. She could have no such luck. She was just the sort of person who worked and worked, day in, day out, week in, week out, without ever finishing. She always had the look of work about her — wet, dirty, unkempt. And all Hammer had to say to get her going was " Isn't it little you've done since morning, Brigid?"

"If I had a proper husband," she would say, " he wouldn't leave all the work to me . . ." And she would go on and on without letting him put in a word.

With most people Hammer usually got the last word in any argument — "Another nail in the plank," except with his wife. In her case, it was always she who drove the nail in the plank, and drove it deep.

Their family had all been reared and scattered, except for one son, who was twenty-seven years old and who would never do any good. It was said that he was mentally retarded, but Brigid loved him more than any of her other sons. She never called him anything except "the creature" and because of this, there were many of the neighbours who did not know his real name, even though they had known him since birth. "Hammer's young fellow" the locals called him. His father disliked him, or pretended to dislike him. (It was said that he considered it a shame for two men in one house to be idle), and lately he had taken to calling him "the Buckeen," on account of the little steel chain he had started wearing. His mother had bought him the chain for a shilling — but that was something that Hammer knew nothing about.

It was the day the chain was bought that I first went to the house. The Big Red-haired Woman had come with me to introduce me to the family. They knew that I was coming, and that the Big Red-haired Woman had undertaken to pay them so much per week for my bed, of which, of course, I had not been told. I had been hoping that they would have given me a little credit, and that I should be able to pay them as soon as I got the job cleaning bottles, which my Red-haired Woman had arranged for me with the owner of that public house where I had first met Little Yellowman.

They gave me a hearty welcome. I should be very comfortable with them. I should have a nice clean bed in the large room, along with six or seven others. — "Lovely boys!" Brigid called them.

"Maybe you'd like a cup of tea now?" asked Brigid.

"We'll all have a cup," said Hammer.

"Put the kettle on the fire," shouted Brigid to someone in another room.

"Surely," answered a voice.

It was a woman's voice, and I thought I recognised it. The

woman came out of the room, laden with tea-things. I was engrossed in debate with Hammer on the Land Question, and did not see her at first. But she saw me, and was so startled to see me that she let all the crockery fall and smash on the floor.

When I heard the crash, I turned around, and I was now the one who was startled.

It was the Fat Lady.

Chapter Twenty-Two

She got a chance to speak to me before I went to bed. She told me her story — all of it that I had not already learned from her letter.

From the time I left the circus, from that night when I started the big rumpus, nothing had gone well for them. Their reputation had suffered. Their best acts left. Little Yellowman himself started to drink . . .

"Where is he now?" I asked, "so that I may catch him, so that I can make him . . ."

"The poor man!" said she.

"Where is he, I say? Where is he?" I asked angrily.

"Beware of him," said she, "beware of him, my dear."

She would not tell me where the scoundrel was. But I could see that she was fully convinced that he meant to kill me. We were sitting on the windowsill outside, so that the people of the house could not hear our conversation. Whenever anybody went past, we had to fall silent until they had gone. At this moment there were some people passing, so that I had to hide my anger.

"Why have you come here?" I asked.

"Since we parted," she said, "since you left me on my own," said she, making sheep's eyes at me, "I couldn't thrive. As I told you in my letter, I kept losing weight daily with loneliness for you . . . eventually I was no longer considered fat enough to be put on show . . . look at me now," said she, standing up, "wouldn't you often see a woman fatter than me?"

She was only telling the truth. There was a street lamp at

her back, so that I had a good view of her. And however she had lost the weight, she had certainly lost a lot, although you could still describe her as a Fat Lady, without doing her any injustice, either.

"Of course, I had to take up some other work," said she, "I am in domestic service here. The people of the house are old friends. And poor old Alf," — she was referring to Little Yellowman — "did his best to cure me. I was given the richest of foods, the strongest of drinks, and plenty of rest and relaxation. But it was no use. I had no appetite, what with fretting for you . . . and if I mentioned your name, he would go out of his mind. Beware of him. Beware of him, I tell you!"

She sat down beside me again. Tears came into her eyes. I thought she was going to kiss and embrace me as she had so often done before, but she only gripped my hand and looked at me with pity in her eyes.

An Italian was passing by with a musical instrument — it was a barrel organ, and he struck up a tune for us.

"In my wildest dreams," she said, holding me in her embrace, "in my wildest dreams, I never expected to be so lucky as to find you here."

"And where did you leave the yellow runt?" I asked.

"The poor man!" said she. "The poor man! How unfortunate he was! What a pitiful state he is in! How sorry I am for him tonight. He has not had peace or rest since that night you created the riot, the poor man! You had no right to do it, when he was only trying to tie the marriage knot between us. You had no right to do it, even if you were a little drunk . . ."

"But what happened to him?"

"Oh, indeed! Nothing happened to him except the break-up of his fine circus that had been over forty years on the road. I wasn't there myself when the final crash came — had I been, it would have broken my heart to see such a fine show being scattered — but every time it was due to open in a town, it would be preceded by letters in the papers announcing to the world how phony his exhibits were. Alas! Those lying letters ruined us."

"And who had been writing the letters?"

"He always thought it was you. That's what made him so bitter towards you."

"He thought it was I?"

"He often said that nobody else but you could have written them. 'The one-legged wretch,' he would say, 'he's the one who's writing them.' But I doubted this. I could not believe that you would wish to destroy the circus while I was in it . . . but he could not be convinced it was not you who were doing the damage . . . he could not.

And, friend of my heart, he went down on his two knees in Sligo and swore that he would have your blood . . . Oh, my dearest! Beware of him — he still has the long knife, ready-sharpened . . ."

"The knife with the bloodstains on it still! Two pence! Two pence each!" said I, imitating Little Yellowman.

"It is no laughing matter," said she, and started to cry, "but you were always laughing at me, — you made a habit of that — but what if he means to kill you? Oh, man! If only you could have seen him! (Her arms stretched above her and her eyes towards the sky). If you had seen him in Sligo on that night we had to leave the city. He went down on his two knees in the centre of the roadway, and started to talk to the long knife, as if it were alive, and swore, 'I said before that you had the trace of blood on you. His blood will be on you before long.' Upon my soul, those were his very words, in the centre of that lonely road in Sligo. Oh man, man! It was terrifying! And the long sharp knife glinting in the moonlight! Alas! Alas!" She began to wring her hands. "It was a terrifying sight. "

I had been trying to cover up a little smile while she was

telling me all this, but, in spite of myself, could suppress it no longer. She saw that smile.

"If you had seen him," she said, with tears in her eyes, "you would not be smiling. You would not be smiling if you knew how worried I have been since I parted from him, in case he should come across you, and stab you to death . . . How often I have wakened up in the middle of the night, pouring with cold sweat, from a terrifying dream. Just a week ago, I had a dream, and you and Alf were in it . . ."

"Stop calling him Alf," said I, "call him little Yellowman." That was the name I liked best for him.

"You and A - a - l . . . and Little Yellowman were in the dream. You were lying on the ground. He was standing over you with the long sharp knife in his hand, just as on that night on the road in Sligo. I screamed, and woke up . . . you were both still before my eyes even though I was now awake. I almost fainted."

She certainly had great love for me. I was trying to puzzle out how she could have come to love a person like me, while the two of us sat there on the windowsill under the light of the street-lamp. I was musing on all the women I had ever known, and on their special qualities. There had been beautiful women and ugly women, women you could love, and women you could not. Why do they give their heart's love to one particular man rather than another? Even though that other might be generally regarded as the better and more handsome man. Except by the woman!

But I expect they see things differently from us. Are there two women alive who would see the same beauty in the one man? . . . If there ever are, that means trouble . . . but I have no solution to that question yet. Not by a long chalk!

I was so lost in thought that I had not noticed the Fat Lady's arm around my neck. Maybe she did not know her arm was there, for she was rapt in thought, staring into the distance. Not at the street lamp beside us, or at the miserable little houses across the road, or at the passers-by, but at something much more beautiful, more ancient, more splendid, so far as she was concerned.

I stirred, and this broke the woman's stream of thought. She drew her arm unobtrusively from around my neck and turned to stare at me as a Guardian Angel might stare at a person who was about to enter an occasion of sin.

"Beware of him, my darling," she said.

I took the pistol I had bought from the sailor out of my pocket.

"I'll be ready for him." I said, showing her the pistol.

I had thought she would be delighted to see that I had a pistol, and that I was ready for him. But may God grant you luck! She was not. She began to cry again, and did not speak for a long time. Some people who were passing by thought that I had done something to make her cry, and stopped to see if they could make peace between us. But, once they saw that there was no argument, they moved on. When speech came to her she started to moan, "Knives and pistols and blood! They mean to kill each other. Oh Lord, what trouble I am in!" I was about to leave when she said "Let me kiss you."

I let her. I was sorry for her. She was so worried and distressed.

I went indoors, and went to bed.

The window beside my bed was just above the one outside which we had been sitting. She was still there. I was unable to sleep for a long time. I tossed and turned from one side of the bed to the other, listening to the snoring of the other people in the room.

Why was she so worried in case anything might happen to little Yellowman? I should have thought she would have been delighted to see him dead. But she wouldn't. Was he also dear to her? After the way he had exploited her? It is hard to comprehend the mind of a woman. How reckless and foolhardy would be the man who tried! She can even show affection for little Yellowman. Why on earth? I shall ask her tomorrow . . .

Well, I said to myself, I shall not be jealous of him, and a smile came to my lips.

I shall question her tomorrow .   .   . to get the matter settled, so as to be perfectly clear about everything.

I heard the Fat Lady going to bed in the room next to us, before I fell asleep.

Chapter Twenty- Three

I was wakened up shortly before ten o'clock, I didn't know what wakened me, for there were only two others in the bedroom, and they both seemed to be sleeping heavily.

I was rubbing my eyes and thinking I might have another little snooze, when there came a measured tapping with a rod at the window beside me. I rose to look out. Who should I see in the window opposite — in the window of her own room — but the Fat Lady, with the rod in her hand.

"Isn't it hard to get you awake?" said she.

"I was in a heavy sleep."

"Here's a cup of tea and a bit of bread for you . . . it will do you good," she said, and she reached them over to me. "I've been trying to waken you for the past half-hour . . . but sure, aren't the other two still asleep?" said she.

"They are — but what was wrong with you not to bring in the tea?" said I.

"God love you!" she said, "you don't know all about this place yet. Don't you know that Brigid has your door locked?"

"The door locked! Why on earth would she want to lock it?"

"In case any of the one-night lodgers should leave without paying . . . but she's coming. I hear her step on the stairs. I'll see you later." And her head disappeared suddenly.

I was drinking my tea and meditating. The two others in the room made an odd movement, and occasionally sighed. Below me in the street people were passing by, passing by all the time. I could hear the voice of Hammer down below. It seemed to me that he was sitting on the same windowsill where the Fat Lady and I had been sitting last night. I was still drinking the tea when I heard; "Another nail in the plank!" I could hear his wife Brigid, too. She was working flat out, but still had time for a snatch of a song now and then. Something like this :

> "I would go to the fair with you
> Eileen Aroon:
> I would go to the fair with you
> Eileen Aroon:
> I would cross the sea over . . . "

When she had sung that much, she would begin the verse again, as if her strenuous work was driving the rest of it out of her mind. I was listening to the Fat Lady, and she was not singing, although she was making a lot of noise, which she was . . .

But how was it that she could have affection for both of us, for both me and Little Yellowman? Could such another woman exist? And the two she loved to be so violently opposed to each other and so unlike in character, in personality, in appearance! If she were to find one attractive, she should surely find the other undesirable. I was puzzled by the situation, but was determined to solve the puzzle. I was worried, but had to laugh at the idea of my taking an interest in her. My interest was not specially in her, but in the situation which was puzzling me . . .

She was outside, waiting to help me down the stairs. "If you have time," I said, "I should like to have a little chat with you in some place where we will not be interrupted."

She was surprised. But if she was, she was also pleased that I was showing that much interest in her, and that I was asking to talk to her, without her having had to ask me first.

About lunchtime, we went to a stable at the back of the lodging-house. There was no horse or other beast in it. I sat on a stone that was keeping the door open. She sat on some hay opposite me. She hadn't an idea in the world what I was going to say to her. She kept her eyes on me, waiting for me to speak, something it took me a while to do. I did not know how to begin.

"You are fond of me," I said at last.

"Don't you know I am?" said she, and a blush came to her cheek.

"And you know that Little Yellowman and I are not friends."

"I know that."

"You are friendly with him. Maybe you prefer him to . . ."

"To anybody else — except yourself," said she.

I was beginning to lose my temper.

"Why are you so fond of him? Don't you know well that he only gave you all those lovely meals to fatten his own pocket? Did he not make you as fat as a- a- a- I don't know what — to make an exhibition of you and money for himself? Have you any shame? Have you any respect for yourself? You disgust me! "

My anger, of course, was not because of what Yellowman had done to her, but because of what he had done to myself.

"I am very fond of him," said she, her head bent, "but I am very fond of you, too."

She surpassed anything I had ever seen before! She was fond of both of us! She would marry us both if she could! But she was ashamed. She still had her head bent down. Surely that was a good sign?

"If you and I were married," said I, to try her out, "would you still love him?"

"I w-w-would," she said.

"And you would love me too, wouldn't you?"

"I would. I would. Very much."

She was to be pitied. I remained silent for a while. I thought she was crying, but she jumped up suddenly, and took hold of my hand. She gripped it so tightly that I was unable to free it from her grasp. She looked at me pitifully. She was moved.

"If I tell you my secret," said she, "will you promise not to reveal it to a living person?"

"I promise."

She was silent for a while, her head down. Then she said :

"He is my father."

I almost fainted.

"But he told me he had never married," said I, as soon as I could speak.

"He hadn't. But it was in this house that I was born and reared until I joined my father's circus," and she explained the whole story, but since it does not specially concern me, I shall not repeat the details here.

When she had told her story, she went off suddenly. I started to meditate, and remained lost in thought for a long time until a cheeky little sparrow, which had been searching for food on the floor, came over to me, and perched on the handle of my crutch, tucked under my shoulder as it was. The conclusion I came to was that I had been completely blind, not to have seen the relationship that existed between Little Yellowman and that Fat Lady he had decided I should marry.

Chapter Twenty-Four

It is now three months since I first came to live in Hammer's lodging-house. I work three days a week in a public house — the same house in which I first met the Big Red-haired Woman. I spend my time down in the cellar, washing bottles and glasses, but they don't pay me very much, since I am missing an arm and a leg.

Since I am free today, I have not bothered to get up. I am lying in bed in the big room, beside the window through which the Fat Lady gave me the cup of tea on my first morning here and, to give her her due, she has not forgotten me any morning since. The summer sun is shining brightly through the window. I hear the small gentle voices of the children playing in the street, and the two men who came in drunk last night do not trouble me, as they are still asleep." Hammer himself is sitting at the front door talking to one of the lodgers. There are seven or eight more of them playing cards and drinking beer in the room next to me. I can hear them swearing and arguing with each other from time to time.

These sheets of paper on which I have been writing are scattered all around me on the bed, but I am unable to continue with my story at present. The thoughts I was hoping to put into words are fast slipping away from me. As if I cannot keep hold of them. I am uncomfortable and dissatisfied with myself and with the world. I am like a wounded lion, or a mountain eagle that has lost the use of its wings, eating my heart out with disappointment and despair at being unable to live my life like a normal human being. How weary I am of this place! How weary I am of the rabble who are Hammer's lodgers! How I detest that crowd who are cursing and swearing in the next room! The small mean ugly streets! The hideous treacherous world that unfolds itself every day before my eyes. The anxiety, the heartache, the weariness, and the deprivation! The poverty that hangs over all, like a great cloud, all the worst sicknesses of body and soul! Lord! If I could only leave it all behind me! If only I could fill my lungs once again with the fresh clean air of Ireland. If I could only feel one tiny breeze from Galway Bay blowing in through this window. But it is not to be. It is unlikely that I shall ever see that great broad bay again, or that city on its shore, or the lake, with its leafy islands, or those mountains I used to see in the distance when I was a child, to marvel at them once more . . . (I shall have to rest: I cannot write a word with the noise, the racket, and the bickering of the card-players) . . . But there is no prison, however confined, without some comfort. Come over here, and take a look at that tall bearded man in the house opposite. I can see him without lifting my head from the pillow. He is going to work. He won't be home till two o'clock in the morning. He is surrounded by his children. He kisses each one tenderly, but gives two kisses to his wife . . . I have noticed him before, whilst I was writing this history, and I was jealous. Jealous because of his happy life, and my unhappy one. When I saw that man, and his wife, and their children, a hundred pictures would come before my eyes. I would see a pretty little house on the edge of a wood; a wife and children there, all full of love and affection for me. How I wished for a life like that enjoyed by the man who lived opposite!

If I were to marry the Fat Lady would she not produce a family for me? Even if I am not in love with her, have not many marriages begun without love? And how often has not love come after marriage? She does not repel me now, as she used to do when we were with Little Yellowman. Certainly, it is not the amount of weight she has lost that has changed my attitude towards her. No, it is the way she keeps doing little things for me. Should I lose a button, who would replace it for me? If my shirt needed washing, who would do it? If it were worn out, who would leave a new one under my pillow? At first, I had disliked her intensely — now, have I not often let her kiss me? . . . Maybe in the future, when I have come to know her better, when we have become used to each other's company, maybe I could come to love her? . . . Next time, instead of waiting for her to kiss me, I shall kiss her first.

That man in the house opposite — he forgot something. I pretended to myself that he had come back to chance seeing his wife again. But he came out with a big sledge-hammer on his shoulder. I was annoyed that it was not to see his wife, as I had been imagining.

But how I hate myself! I don't deserve God's blessing. Am I not just as bad as those romantic authors who thought that there was nothing in the world but sunshine and fine green fields where daisies and marigolds and Our Lady's thimbles nod their heads in conclave with every breeze that blows? Was I not equally mistaken, making up a false romance about that bearded man who only came back for his sledge-hammer; just as mistaken as those poets whose life and work were filled with illusory dreams, with Muses who never existed and Venuses who were never in the skies?

I wish those card players would choke. Why won't they allow me to record my thoughts? It's no use; I can write no more today, with the noise they are making.

I can hear the soft voices of the children playing together below me in the street. I shall go down among them and tell them a story.

* * * * *

I am sitting on the footpath at the side of the street, out in front of Hammer's house. The children are gathered around me. Almost a hundred of them. The lodging-house windows are open, and I can see everything inside, including the card players. But the little ones around me take no notice of the rotting old house that is falling asunder from old age, or of the card-players swearing and drinking beer at the window, or of Hammer putting "another nail in the plank" or of the ugly little street, or of the filthy smell that comes on the wind. They are far away from the place; in a beautiful distant land, where children are never hungry, or men angry, or the hearts of women treacherous.

". . . and the King's son went into that enchanted wood, where he met a beautiful young maiden . . ."

I heard the words I was saying, but the King's son and the maiden did not have time to become acquainted, before another of Hammer's lodgers, a man called King-Kong, came to tempt some of my audience away. His pockets were full, and he started to distribute apples among the smaller children.

He is a strange man, certainly. He is learned, and they say he once held an important position, but spent five years in prison, and when he came out, was unable to find any employment. However, a brother of his sends him a weekly allowance — thirty shillings every Saturday. His two greatest qualities are his love for children and his knowledge of languages.

"Carry on," he said to me, "my friends won't understand your story. They are not old enough yet."

". . . and the maiden spoke to the King's son, and told him where the magic tree was, with the golden apples, and they went away, hand in hand, until they reached the tree . . ."

Some of the children who were with King-Kong were disappointed that he was not giving them more apples.

Once in a while, a tiny little hand would slip into the apple pocket, but he would pretend not to notice the hand was there until an apple had been taken out. Then he would pounce on the hand, take the apple, and give it to another child. He never had enough apples for all the children, so that there was always a scramble while he was sharing them out!

I was never able to do much with King-Kong's crowd of youngsters. They were too young to understand the stories, and they were also afraid of me, my face was so twisted and scarred, but even so, occasionally, a brave little one would come over to me, and stick a curly head under my arm, his mouth sticky from sweets.

". . . There was a good strong wind blowing that day, and the beautiful maiden and the King's son stood under the tree, where they heard music sweeter than was ever heard by human ear, before or since, as the golden apples tinkled against each other . . ."

A light appeared in the eyes of the children as they listened to me, the light which is the reward of the storyteller. All I needed was to see that light, and I knew then that they were listening to the music of the golden apples, and not to the melodeon being played in Hammer's lodging-house. And every time I saw that light in the children's eyes, I knew that they could see the same light in mine, and were filled with wonder.

The King's son had not succeeded in picking many of the golden apples, when I was suddenly interrupted. I hear someone calling me loudly:

"Michael ! Michael!"

I raised my head, and who should I see, in a window of the lodging-house but the Big Red-haired Woman.

"Michael ! Michael !"

"I won't keep you a minute." I shouted.

"Hurry up! Hurry up! I have important news!"said she.

I had intended to finish the children's story first, but she wouldn't let me. I had to go in. The gamblers heard the talk, and started to laugh at us. As I went up the stairs, I heard one of them starting to tell a story (one which I had to listen to one morning when Brigid had locked us in the bedroom), a story too obscene to be told anywhere except in the depths of Hell.

I was glad when I saw one or two of the card-players out in the street some time later. They hadn't waited for the story.

Chapter Twenty-Five

The Big Red-haired Woman opened the door to me. "Sit down there," she said, rudely. I sat on the chair. I looked at her. In my time, I had often seen a person in a rage, but never before in a rage like this. Her eyes were on fire. There was a storm in her face. There was madness in her voice.

"And you are to be married!" said she, trying, but failing, to sound casual and innocent.

I looked at her again. I looked around the room. The Fat Lady was sitting shivering in the corner of the room furthest from me. Her face was as white as driven snow, and she was in a cold sweat.

"And you are to be married!" said the Big Red-haired Woman again.

"I admire your choice," she said, keeping her anger in check.

The Fat Lady made as if to say something, but the other woman just looked at her. She kept silent.

"And they thought to do it without our knowing — not even an invitation to the wedding!" said she. She sounded mocking, but it was the mockery of anger.

"Who told you I was to be married?" I asked, "And if I am, where's the woman?"

"There she is, over there," said she, "and a fine stout woman she is, too, may God and Mary and the people bless her."

I almost laughed, but I was a little afraid of her. And if I were going to marry the Fat Lady, what business had she to come between us? What had it to do with her? Why should I not marry her if I wished? But . . . maybe the Big Red-haired woman is in love with me herself!

She spoke again.

"Come here, my dear," said she to the Fat Lady, "and give him a kiss."

The Fat Lady started. You would think somebody had stuck a pin in her bottom. She didn't get up.

"Aren't you the shy one?" said the big Red-haired Woman, sarcastically, "but don't I know you both well of old?"

The other woman didn't move. She looked as if she were going to faint.

"I'll look out the window," said the Red-haired Woman, "so that I won't see you at all. Now."

She went to the window, and looked out. Certainly she loved me, and was jealous of the other woman. I thought I could get some fun out of her.

"Come over here," I said to the other woman," and sit beside me."

"Do," said the woman at the window, without looking at us.

The Fat Lady got up and came over to me slowly. She sat on a chair beside me.

"Give me a kiss, now, darling," said I, "just one."

The woman at the window was visibly angry. I saw her clenching her two fists, but wasn't it she who had told me to kiss the Fat Lady?

"Just one kiss, my dear," said I, as affectionately as I could. I was afraid I should burst out laughing. But the Fat Lady thought I was in earnest. She bent over me. She gave me the kiss, but, if she did, the other woman gave her a box on the ear and knocked her to the floor.

"I am ashamed of you! Ashamed!" I said to the Big

Red-haired Woman.

"Get up," said she to the woman who was sitting on the floor, "get up, or I'll . . ."

She got up.

"Go over there and stay where I put you!"

The Fat Lady went over. Then the other woman turned to me.

"It would take little to persuade me to give you the same treatment," said she. "Only for your condition, you would not escape. To think that a son of your father and mother would do such a thing! Would marry the showman's daughter! Marry her! Look at her! Just look at her!"

"Can't I marry whoever I choose?" said I, teasing her.

"Oh, yes, yes," said she, sniggering.

The Fat Lady opened her mouth to speak. The other woman looked at her. Her mouth remained open. The card-players were singing songs; the children were playing on the street; Hammer was debating at the door; and here was I, contending with the two women in the room, although I wasn't, really, but having a bit of fun for myself. A pair of women quarrelling over me! Over someone like me! And what a pair! Who would have thought it of the Big Red-haired Woman? Who would have thought she had anything but motherly love for me? But no. If it were only that, would she be upset by the idea of my marrying the other woman? She was jealous. I pretended to have great affection for the Fat Lady; you would have thought by me that I loved her more than any woman who ever lived. She supposed that I was in earnest, and even though she was nervous, she was delighted that the Big Red-haired Woman had not succeeded in getting me to break off the engagement. And, of course, the Red-haired Woman believed the engagement was still on, which was what I wanted her to believe. What fun I was having!

"Are you agreeable to break off this engagement with the

showman's daughter?" asked the Big Red-haired Woman.

"I am not," I said.

"Will you break off the engagement?" she asked for the second time.

"I will not," I said boldly.

"Will you break it off?" she asked, for the third time.

"I will not," I said, and felt like laughing.

She said nothing more, but went to the door and called Brigid. She came.

"Give me the key," said the Big Red-haired Woman.

"Isn't it time . . ?" said Brigid, but the Big Red-haired woman interrupted her before she could finish.

"Give me the key," said she, threateningly.

She got it, and went out, locking the door behind her.

"This engagement will be broken off tonight," she said as she went out, "I swear it!"

I burst out laughing. Laughing at the whole idea that she should think I meant to marry the Fat Lady, that the Fat Lady believed it herself. But why had she locked the door on us?

The Fat Lady came over to me. She sat down beside me. She was gentle and affectionate. I thought she was going to stand up and start kissing me against my will as she had so often done before. Love was shining in her eyes.

"I thought you would give in," she said, "I was terrified you would give in to her," said she.

"That I would give in?" I asked.

"Yes — and break off our engagement," said she.

"There was little danger of that," I said.

"I knew that, my dear, as soon as I saw you letting her lock the door."

"But why did she lock the door?" I asked.

"Oh, do you not know — to keep us both locked in here until your people come!"

"Until my people come?"

"Yes, did you not know she had sent for them?" said she "Don't you know that your uncle and his daughter will be here within a few hours? They have been searching for you ever since the riot at the circus in Galway. It was the Red-haired Woman who told them where you were, and told them of your unfortunate circumstances . . . "

"And my uncle and his daughter will be here in a few hours, you say," I said, quietly and easily, although my heart was beating fast.

"They will. Did the Red-haired Woman not tell you?"

I did not answer. I was bewildered. There are people in the world who, when in trouble, will look for help from their relatives. I have never been one of those people. No matter how badly things were ever going for me, I had always sent good reports home to my family. But I was now disgraced. They would know all about me. Had I been aware that they knew my story, I should have made certain they didn't find me.

"And she told them of the sorry state I am in here?" said I.

"She did."

"And she told them that I had been in Galway and all over Ireland as a freak and a horror and a public spectacle with your yellow rogue of a father; did she tell them that?"

"She did."

"And of the time I spent wandering about without a bit of food to put in my stomach; that she fed me herself when I had almost starved to death — did she tell them all that?"

"She did."

"And, worst of all, I suppose she told them I was engaged — engaged to be married to a woman who had been on exhibition all her life and who was twenty-seven stone weight!"

"Oh, Michael, Michael, I was never twenty-seven stone; I was not, Michael, I was not. It was my father who used to say that . . ."

"Did she tell them?"

"She did."

"And who told her there was an engagement?" I said fiercely. The fun was over.

"But isn't there, Michael? Wasn't the match made that day in Galway long ago? I knew you were willing when you kissed me last Sunday — you kissed me of your own free will, of your own free will, Michael . . . I thought you were only waiting for me to have the money put together. I told her we were to be married, Michael.

She went into a rage. She nearly killed me, Michael — she was like a lunatic. She thought to break up the engagement. She said you would be ashamed in front of your family . . . that you would be ashamed of me, Michael, and that you would never marry me. She locked the door so that we should be seen together . . . expecting you to be ashamed . . . but I knew you wouldn't be; didn't you let her do it?"

She grasped my hand when she had said this much. But I pulled my hand away. I grabbed the door-knob, and started to shake it. The Red-haired Woman had locked it tight. We were in prison together. When the card-players heard me shaking the door, they started to laugh and jeer us. They were having great fun.

I was losing my temper. I had got myself into this fix. It had started as a laugh and a joke. I pretending that I meant to marry the Fat Lady. The other woman jealous, as I thought. Trying, in fact, to break up a non-existent engagement. But I was now disgraced. I should never be able to set foot in my native city again. The town children would follow me with their eyes as I went down the street, and tell each other that they had seen me on exhibition as a freak and a madman. Mothers would frighten their children with the story that I had a long sharp knife with the traces of blood on it in my pocket. And what would my own cousin Mary think, she whom I had intended to marry before I first left Galway, when she saw the woman I now meant to marry?

I grabbed the door-knob again and shook it. It was no use. I could not leave the room. The door was heavy. The lock was strong. I should have to wait until they came.

I sat beside the window. Could I climb out that way? No, not even if I had the use of my limbs.

"Michael! Michael!" said the Fat Lady, moving towards me.

"Stay away from me," I said, "or . . ."

She came no nearer. What a remarkable courtship it was! Here was I sitting beside the window, my heart swollen with shame and disappointment and bad temper. She sitting on the bed, crying because I was not speaking to her, because I was not being friendly, was not glad to be in her company, and without her knowing why I was so unhappy.

It is snowing. There is a noble white carpet spread over the dirty ugly streets and the ancient houses that are falling apart from old age. There is not a sound to be heard in the lodging-house. The lodgers are all drinking in the public house across the way. I am sitting here beside the window looking over at them, and waiting for my relatives to arrive. The woman is sitting on the bed weeping quietly. She speaks:

"I have a key, if you want to go before they come. If you are ashamed . . . that your relatives . . . should see . . . me."

The tears were blinding her and preventing her from speaking.

"I don't want to leave."

"If I . . . go . . . with . . . you . . . Michael?"

"Come on," I said, taking hold of her arm, "let's go."

We went down quietly. Nobody stopped us.

We went out onto the street.

Chapter Twenty-Six

It was Saturday night when I eloped with the Fat Lady and the neighbours were celebrating their Saturnalia. The people had their week's wages, and they were spending them. There would be trouble and strife before the night was over. I had the woman. But why had I brought her with me? What should I do with her? Bring her back to the lodging-house? Or marry her?

It was a problem that I couldn't solve on the spot. All I did was go into a public house to drink a pint with my sweetheart. And she was so full of joy and pride that she had got me at last!

Yes, it was out of hatred and spite for my uncle and for that Mary Lee, who would not marry me when I was a strong and handsome youth, that I was now eloping with the Fat Lady. I suppose they have arrived in the lodging-house by now. Won't Mary be surprised when she sees the place? What will she say to Hammer and his wife, and to the lodgers? What will she think of the present way of life of the young man she once loved? What opinion will she have of the woman he is now going to marry? The same opinion as he has of the man she herself married, perhaps. But she will not see her . . . .

(The woman beside me was gazing rapturously at me while my thoughts were running on like this) . . . I should love you to see her, Mary. Oh, if you could only see her! You would know then that I am independent of all of you.

"Did you bring your photograph?" I asked the woman beside me.

" I didn't. I hadn't time."

"It's still hanging on the wall, then?" said I.

"It is. Isn't it a pity? My lovely photograph.Wasn't I looking beautiful the day it was taken? I have never looked better!"

She had never looked fatter! Wouldn't Mary be horrified when she saw her?

But it is getting late. The racket is beginning. The singsong, the shouting, the commotion are under way. Men and women, old and young, are being thrown out of the public houses. Cursing and swearing. Obscenities flying through the air, like flames from the mouths of demons. The soft sweet voices of the children. The high voices of the screeching women, the fierce rough voices of the men fighting.

"I shall have to pay a visit to John MacDonagh before I leave the neighbourhood," I said to the Fat Lady.

"Shall I wait for you here?"

"No. Come with me."

We went off through the snow.

John was a young man who took a great interest in the Irish language. Only for him I should not be able to write a word; I should not be covering paper with these adventures. He had a big room on rent, and any Irishman was welcome there. He hadn't known much of the language when he first took the room, but had learned a lot from the old men who came to visit him every night.

We reached the house. We climbed the stairs, and looked in through the glass door of the big room. We both almost collapsed. For who were there but my uncle and Mary and the Big Red-haired Woman and Little Yellowman — all talking to John. When my companion caught sight of her father, she disappeared in a flash, terrified that he should take her away with him. But I stayed at the door looking in.

Mary Lee was standing in the middle of the floor, looking at her father, who was sitting in a big chair beside the fire.

That gentleman was staring at little Yellowman, his eyes full of surprise. The Red-haired Woman was also staring at him, surprise in her eyes too. The talk was coming out of Little Yellowman in torrents. Now and again, Mary Lee opened her mouth to speak, but could not get a word in edgeways. Oh! If she had known that I was at the door, and that I was so impatient to hear her voice!

"It's my daughter I want," Little Yellowman was saying, "I want my daughter, and won't leave this house till I see her. Who stole her from me? Who stole her? Where have you hidden her? I was told she was here. That she has been seen in the company of that cursed devil who ruined my fine circus . . . that he was forcing her to marry him . . . where have you hidden them?"

He began to search the room. He searched here, he searched there. He searched under the table, under the chairs, everywhere, talking all the time. He was still the same little Yellowman. It seemed to me that he looked a bit shook; that he had not that prosperous appearance he had when I first met him. But he still had the long hooked nose, and the little pointed chin, which kept trying to kiss each other as he talked.

The Red-haired Woman had the little picture I mentioned before. She handed it to Mary Lee.

"And is that she?" asked Mary, horrified.

Little Yellowman came over to her. He grabbed the photograph, and started kissing it.

"My daughter! my fine beautiful daughter! That kind gentle lady, as innocent as an unborn child."

Mary Lee gave a little laugh. Whether she was laughing at myself and my bride-to-be, or at little Yellowman's expense, I couldn't tell, but she annoyed me intensely.

"I tell you she's not here," said the Red-haired Woman, "Didn't I put them under lock and key until these good people should arrive . . . ?"

"Where is she? Where is she?" Little Yellowman was saying. "That venomous thief has stolen my precious jewel, my shining star, my best in the world, and you people are helping him . . . Oh! Am I not to be pitied tonight?"

He sat heavily on a chair. He held his head in his hands, and began to sway from side to side.

My uncle had the little photograph by now, and kept looking at it. Now and again a twinkle of humour would come into his eyes, but it would disappear again as quickly .

"I have always said there was an odd streak in him," he said quietly to his daughter. "He got it from his father's people."

"If there wasn't, he wouldn't be so crazy as to be marrying her," said the daughter, looking at the photograph.

"And the poor man was a hard worker in his day."

"He was," said the daughter . . . "and but for me, he would have stayed at home."

"It was his fate," said her father.

"He must have been very attracted to her, to abduct her from her father like that," said she.

They looked over at the "poor father," who was distraught with worry for his daughter, if he was to be believed. They felt sorry for him. I was certain they must think me a consummate devil, a blackguard who had deprived him of his livelihood, had stolen his daughter, and had left him in poverty. I was wondering what would be my best method of letting them know that I was in no way dependent on them, and that I had no regard for them or for their opinion. That feeling of shame that came over me when I was first afraid that they would hear the story, and make me an object of derision in my native town, had now completely left me. I should never again be able to set foot on my own country. I, who had taken a handful of Irish sand in my fist that day when I landed on Waterford quay with little Yellowman, and crushed it until the blood seeped through the skin, I should now have to remain forever away from the land I loved best in the world. But I planned to get satisfaction, to have my revenge on those who were the cause of my misfortunes; to damage their reputation somehow, to humble them, to shame them, to put them down . . .

The Fat Lady came up to the top of the stairs to see what I was doing. I motioned her to come with me. A crowd of men and women were passing by in the street, singing. I could tell by their voices that they were half-drunk. I knew that some of them were Hammer's lodgers. I told the Fat Lady to call them. She did. They came over to me, at least ten of them, men and women, all carrying cans of beer, all wet from the snow, all ragged and foul-mouthed. The Fat Lady put her arm in mine; somebody opened the door for us, and we went in.

The crowd followed.

Chapter Twenty-Seven

Everything that had befallen me, from the time I first left home to earn a little money so as to be able to marry Mary Lee, now came before my eyes. The accident that had left me a cripple and a freak; my shameful life with little Yellowman; the match he had first made for me; my poverty and hunger and need, whilst I was waiting for my money; how the Red-haired Woman had come to my rescue; Hammer's lodging-house, full of thieves and blackguards; how I had been compelled to sit at table there with the dregs of the city; how I had been pursued by the Fat Lady; I could see all this and more, coming and going, in the clearest of pictures.

I knew that my uncle was an honest respectable man. I knew how he despised drunkards. He had little regard for anyone who was not as well-off as himself. And a rich man, in his estimation, was always one to be admired. His daughter Mary, who had once loved me so dearly, did not share his views, but had some of the same stuff in her.

I had decided to shame them both. I would let them know what I thought of them.

"This is the woman I am going to marry," I said, when they spoke to me.

They looked in horror at the pair of us. They said nothing, but greeted the Fat Lady with respect.

Little Yellowman was a short distance away from us, being held back by John MacDonagh and the Red-haired Woman. "Where's my knife? Where's my knife, I say, till I stick it to the handle in him?" he roared. His daughter was behind me, shaking all over, but, to give her her due, she plucked up her courage quickly. She came between me and Yellowman. "You will have to stick it in me first," she said, putting out both arms to protect me.

My uncle and his daughter were looking at the crowd who had come in with us.

"They have come to the wedding," I told them; "They are friends of mine," said I, " I'll introduce them to you."

They did not protest. They were too polite. But I thought that Mary Lee was ready to cry with petulance to be in such company.

"King-Kong," I called.

That individual came up, and bowed politely to them.

"You learned French in the Convent," I said to Mary Lee.

King-Kong tried to speak a little French, but was too drunk to speak any language.

He had to sit down.

"This is Mr. Friel, or 'Wait a bit,' as they call him," said I.

My uncle and his daughter bowed.

"If you want a fighting man, send for Mr. Friel," I explained.

"James Sheehan," I called, and a big powerful man came over. He looked as if he could knock down the house if he had a mind to.

They bowed to him.

"Welcome. Welcome, my dear lady. You have come to the wedding too, I take it?"

That was the first word spoken, and the last, until I had introduced everybody there in as polite and as gracious a manner as if I were at a Royal reception.

"Now you know, Mary," said I, "that I am not short of friends in this country."

"And what dreadful people," she said, under her breath.

"It's a dreadful world," said her father, "I should never have believed I should find my brother's son in such a place and in such company. Never . . . Oh, if your mother were alive . . . Michael!"

"Yes."

"You should come home with us . . ."

"I'm fine here. Am I not to be married . . .? "

"What attraction has she for you? Have you any sense Michael? — and Michael," he repeated in a friendly tone,"if you want to get married, Michael, I'll get you a woman in Galway, a fine young woman . . ."

"I thought I had found a fine young woman there long ago," said I, "but I didn't succeed. She married another," and I looked at Mary.

They both remained silent. Yellowman was trying to get at me all the time, but two people were holding him back. The people whom I had brought in to introduce to my relatives were chatting contentedly about the wedding.

I came face to face with Yellowman. I put my hand into my trousers pocket, and took out the pistol I had bought long ago from the sailor. I adopted an aggressive posture.

"You rotten thief," I said, threateningly, "where is my money?"

The whole crowd gathered around us. They grabbed hold of the two enemies.

"Take his pistol," said one.

"Take his knife," said another.

The riot began. Everybody was putting in his oar. My uncle and his daughter cowered to one side, terrified. The Fat Lady stood between the two of us, screaming.

"Knives and pistols and blood!" she was screaming. "Knives and pistols, and they mean to kill each other. They have me tormented!" she kept saying.

But the Big Red-haired Woman came down like a mountain torrent tumbling down from snowy peaks, and sweeping all before her.

"Only I'm reluctant to do it, I'd grab you both by the back

of the head and throw you out the window. Aren't you the fighting men? Aren't you the great heroes?"

Things quietened down. I glanced over at Mary. She was shivering. She would have preferred to be anywhere else but in the place she was.

I went over to her.

"Were you going to kill the poor old man?" she asked.

"I shall kill him yet . . . ."

"Don't say such a thing, Michael."

"I wouldn't say it, or do it, if he did not deserve it, the devil!" said I, looking over at him. He looked back at me, and it was not a pleasant look.

"Michael," said the woman beside me, with her hand on my shoulder, "Michael!" said she.

"Yes."

"What a great change has come over you, Michael," she said, looking at me sadly.

"What change?" said I, skittishly, "except that I'm older, that I have only one leg, and one arm, and that I am not as handsome as I was when you used to find me attractive, when I left my home town to earn a little money . . ."

There were tears in her eyes. She tried to keep them back, but did not succeed very well.

"Are you still as fond of the money as ever?" I asked suddenly.

The tears came. I had no sympathy for her. I didn't care how I might hurt her.

"The man you married had plenty of money," said I, "I should never have been able to earn that much, with all the will in the world . . ."

I was unable to finish what I was saying. She began to cry bitterly. I was delighted that I had succeeded in drawing tears from this fine lady who had ruined my life. Only for the cursed passion for money of her father and herself, I should have had a different tale to tell. A match had been made for her with an upstart who had nothing to his credit but his money, something that I never had, until I got the two hundred and fifty pounds out of the accident. . . .

"Shut up," she said, interrupting me angrily.

I tried to continue, but she turned on me.

"Shut up," she said again, "and don't speak ill of the dead . . . may the Lord rest his soul."

"And is he dead?" I asked, dumbfounded.

"Did you not hear about it?"

"Not a word. If I had . . ."

"He was killed nine months ago. He fell from his horse on his way to the fair."

We were both silent. Yellowman was in a corner with my uncle. John MacDonagh and the Red-haired Woman were in another corner with two or three other people. The crowd who had come in were getting merry. A woman here drinking beer. A man there playing music. Another saying what a great match it was. The snow spattering softly against the window. Angry voices, murmuring voices, rough strident voices coming from the street. The woman I had once meant to marry, now a widow, sitting beside me; the woman I now meant to marry, against my better judgment, sitting by herself, looking over at us.

It was Mary who spoke first.

"Never a day passed, Michael, since you left Galway," she said, with a tremor in her voice, "since that first day you left, that I have not prayed to God for you."

Her hand was on my shoulder again. She was looking at me lovingly.

"Do you ever say a prayer for me?" she asked, "Have you ever asked God to set me on the right path?"

"If there were a God," said I.

She took her hand from my shoulder, and drew a little away from me.

"Oh, you are greatly changed," said she, "I was

unfortunate to have ever allowed you to leave . . . may God forgive me for it . . ."

A man at the top of the room started to sing a song. I signalled to the Fat Lady to come over to me. Somebody placed a chair for her beside me. Mary Lee went over to her father. Music struck up. The singing began. The wedding feast was in full swing.

* * * * *

And it was in full swing when I slipped away. Nobody heard me going out. Even if they had, it would not have occurred to them that I didn't mean to come back. My relatives were unlikely to take much interest in me for the future. Hadn't I shown them what I thought of them? Treating Mary Lee to that kind of company! A fine lady like her! How stupid I had been to think that I should be ashamed in front of them. It is they who should be ashamed! Only for them, I should not be in this sorry state tonight.

I moved off through the snow as fast as I was able, overjoyed that I had humbled them, insulted them, shamed them.

But what's this? A grimy back-street. Snow churned into mud under people's feet. Everything a grey colour. A gathering of men, women and children. They are very excited. Terrified. Disturbed.

A young woman is lying on the dirty grey slush. She doesn't stir. There is a man standing by her, a huge sledge-hammer on the ground beside him. He is half-drunk; five men are holding him; some of them want to kill him straight away. The woman on the snow is his wife. The sledge-hammer on the ground is his (was he not seen carrying it this morning?), and if the woman isn't dead, the new-born baby is . . .

A doctor and a policeman arrived. The wretch was arrested. The half-dead woman was taken away. The infant was wrapped in a sheet and taken to the morgue.

It has started to snow again, but there is no sign of the people going away. They seem to be stuck to the place, and the crowd is getting bigger. The ones who are half-drunk are beginning to sober up. The police are having to keep them away from the spot where the woman has fallen in the snow. They are discussing the dreadful deed which has been done.

And before the man and the woman and the dead baby who was born in the snow were taken away, I imagined that the little lighted windows in the small dark houses on each side were like the eyes of some evil beast that did not like the human race. And didn't those eyes look mockingly at the little knot of people in their wet rags, at the woman who lay half-dead in the snow, at the infant who had never seen the light, and at the drunken father whom the police had arrested? . . .

I was filled with dread.

I felt in my heart that a foul deed, a dreadful deed had been done on the spot where I was. I could not stay there any longer. The power of the deed that had been done, which was driving me away from the place, was drawing thousands more towards it. All I wanted was to get as far away as I could. To sever all connection with the horrible life I had been leading for so long. To leave the Fat Lady far behind me. Had I married her, it is certain I should have killed her, just as that drunken beast has killed his wife.

Passing by the hospital, I saw a young boy standing outside the door in the snow. He was weeping bitterly; I recognised him. Had I not often told a story to himself and his little companions? . . . The son of the man who used to kiss his wife twice every morning, the son of that man who had killed his wife with the sledge-hammer.

The young fellow followed his mother's body through

the hospital door. . . .

I shambled away from the place, and the devil was eating my heart.

Chapter Twenty-Eight

Spring has not yet arrived, but my friends and I are looking forward to its coming. On the night of the murder I didn't travel very far from the scene. I stopped at the park where the poor wretches lying on the grass had seemed like a diseased giant.

They are still there. But this time I do not see them as black spots on the flesh of the giant. No, they are more like jelly-fish left on a beach by the tide. As if they had been waiting for a very long time for the tide to come in again and float them away. But are they really waiting for a tide? Hardly. They are, if the truth be told, waiting for the coming of spring, the season of renewal and of hope for the future. Waiting for the sun to restore warmth to their bones and for the coming of the season when they can again move freely around the country as independent as kings.

Until that season comes, they and I will have to remain here, waiting. But, unless God should intervene, I shall have to stay here for the rest of my life. If I only had the use of my legs! The use of my legs! Isn't that a peculiar phrase? But when a person is hungry, afraid, and peevish in himself, forced to spend his nights outdoors in rain and cold, with little to cover him, he will not worry so much over his past misfortunes, as over his present sorry situation. If I even had the use of my legs I could at least take to the roads as vigorously as any of these vagrants who now surround me, and who have the same instinct to travel as a flock of migratory birds.

It was only when spring came and I saw them all

preparing to leave, that I fully realised the extent of my disability. Oh! If I could only get out of this accursed city!

Spring is here today for certain. The sun is smiling in the sky like an indulgent mother whose only wish is to comfort and care for her children. The water in that pool over there, which was covered with ice a fortnight ago, is now like a lake of silver dancing in the sunshine! And the South wind! How lovely it is! Even in the city it is welcome. The sap is rising in the trees. There is not a corner in the park that is not bursting with growth and new life. Lying here on the grass, among the vagrants, I imagine that a keen-eyed person could almost see the grass growing. I lay my head back on the ground .   .   . Something fell on my nose. I took hold if it. A long slender green insect that had wakened from its winter sleep. I felt my own heart leaping. My spirits rose. I laid the long slender insect on a withered leaf that had lain on the ground through the winter. I was examining it carefully. Some of the other poor people saw me. They gathered around. Perhaps it was a coin that I had found on the grass. They started to search, themselves. At first I didn't hear them. Then I was surprised at the fuss that was going on around me. And they heard me say; "God is strong."

There was an old man there who had a saintly appearance. He would have reminded you of Michelangelo's Moses, with his long white beard, and his noble features .   .   . but when he heard my remark, he began to blaspheme and curse and swear. He swore that Satan had taken charge of the world. That God had been dead for years. A red rag would not have angered a bull more than the name of God enraged this starving white-bearded old man who had such a look of Moses.

Some of them agreed with him, and were ready to strike me. There were others there who thought that I was mocking them. Others were simply disappointed that it was not money I had found, and that they still had nothing, after my raising their hopes. They were threatening. All were annoyed with me, and they drove me from the park.

Stop deceiving yourself, Michael. Stop pretending to yourself that you are not starving with hunger. What good will that do you? Even though you have eaten a morsel of bread and meat left behind by a workman in a public house, what use is that? Haven't you already digested every scrap that is in your stomach? You have no use tightening your belt around your waist. You have already tightened it three times. And if your appearance gives the impression of hunger and poverty, what chance will you have of getting that little job you have been promised?

The prospect of that job had been occupying my mind for a number of days. I should make a good watchman. I should need to be sharp-eyed and far-sighted so as not to be sacked. I should get a comfortable little lodging. I should have a little room to myself. I should be able to keep my books and papers there. There would be clean wholesome food ready for me when I came home after the night. The Fat Lady? Wasn't I lucky I didn't marry that woman? They will surely leave me be from now on .   .   .

George Fott, I applaud you. But for you, good George, I should be a long time waiting for a job. Here's wishing you prosperity, George. May you find a wife to your liking, George! May your children respect you! Tomorrow night I shall be starting as your watchman. My misery will be a thing of the past. It will be the beginning of a new life.

I stared into a pool to check on my appearance. It seemed all right. I thought I was looking well. Once I was getting the pound a week, I should be able to buy myself clothes. A pound a week! A man could not marry on it .   .   .   but if the wife were earning too? If she were getting another pound, we should have a good life, and I should not be too old as my children grew up around me. I am still not thirty years old .   .   .   if we had the two pounds a week between us, we should have no difficulty in saving a little money every week. We might even succeed in putting enough aside to bring us to Ireland on a summer holiday. Ten pounds would do this .   .   . but I should not be able to visit my native town until everybody had forgotten my exploits while I was touring with Little Yellowman.

Wasn't I lucky I didn't marry his daughter?

The wife that I shall have (the wife that I have, I should more properly say, for I already have her in my dreams); my chosen wife would be tall and dark; her eyes as black as sloes; her cheeks the colour of the rose; and her lips .   .   . I thought about every beautiful woman who had lived since Helen of Troy, and was convinced that there was never one so noble, so lovely, as this wife of mine - this wife I possessed in my dreams. I forgot my hunger. I should be independent of this miserable life. Had I not the comfort of this beautiful company of women? Did they not speak with me? And that wonderful conversation I had with the woman for whom Troy was devastated. She was delighted to hear that her name was still on people's lips, and delighted that I had been thinking of her. "My name will be in songs," said she, "until the end of time," and she vanished on the wind.

Then came Deirdre, Naoise's lover, as I lay on my back in the park .   .   . but it was not the tragic Deirdre, but a proud and glorious one, and when I thought to ask her about the sons of Uisneach, she disappeared. Beautiful women who had brought down kingdoms passed across the skies above me: Gormfhlaith of the Irish and Doña Elvira of the Spaniards were part of this sad company; beautiful women who had saved their countries —   Joan of Arc on her white horse, sword in hand, along with many others whom I did not recognise. Queen Maedhbh was there, and Cleopatra of Egypt, both triumphant and proud, along with arrogant conceited women — women who had been the cause of conflict and slaughter in attempting to enforce their will on others.

The important people who were passing by in their fine shiny coaches did not see any of them. The cripple saw them, and only he.

But, Michael, you will have to chase away these dreams, or you will not get this job from Fott. Away with you, Helen of Troy! Be gone, Maedhbh and Cleopatra! . . . Why are you delaying there? Don't you know that I shall have to wash myself in the lake down there, and that I shall have to wash my clothes so as to appear presentable when I go to see George Fott to take up this position.

I am in a hurry. Be off with you, I say, but you may come back — as soon as I have got the job.

*   *   *   *   *

My curse upon you, George Fott! The curse of the saints on you, George! The curse of the angels on you, George! The curse of the weak on you! The curse of the strong! The curse of the friars, the curse of the priests, the curse of the bishops, you lying George Fott! The curse of the mothers on you, George! The curse of their children! May life go hard with you, and may the gravestone lie heavy on your head!

What good advice you gave me, Fott of ill omen! To go to the poor-house! And what made you think that it was advice that I needed from you? Did you think that I had put that noble company to flight just to go to you for advice, you treacherous Fott? There was a time when you would not have lived any longer had you given me advice like that, George. But things have changed with me. I no longer have the energy to strike a man, or the courage. All I can do is curse you — my curse upon you, George Fott! . . .
Maybe my curse might have more effect were I to write it down on paper . . . and I have written it here, sitting

under an oak tree, in the middle of a park, in London, England, on this beautiful spring morning on the nineteenth day of April in the year nineteen hundred and seven.

I am waiting for the return of the pleasant company that I had sent away so as to visit George Fott. But they are not coming back; nothing is coming except gloomy thoughts, dark gloomy thoughts, and the delirium of hunger . . .

But the dark thoughts do not torment me all the time. I got a couple of pence yesterday for holding a horse and I bought a bit of cheese and some bread. I drank a glass of beer. I went into the park and sat under the oak tree. A kind of merriment came into my heart. I could feel the blood coursing through my veins. There were a lot of people in the park, but they had no notion of how happy was the cripple who was singing heartily under the oak tree.

This poor man was found dead under an oak tree, in the middle of a park, in London, England. Some of these pages were in his pocket. There was a pistol beside him which had never been fired. It was only a toy which had failed the man who carried it. Beside him also was an old knife, an old blunt chipped knife — the knife that had killed him.

. . . And little had my poor friend thought that the pistol bought from the sailor would fail him — but had not life itself failed him?